The Visitor Series

The Visitor

Meets
Old Hairy

Book 2 by Fay Lamb

Write Integrity Press

The Visitor Meets Old Hairy
Copyright: ©2023 Fay Lamb

ISBN: 978-1-951602-20-8

Published by Pursued Books: an imprint of

P Write Integrity Press, LLC
PO Box
Dallas, TX 75370

Printed in the United States of America

Dedication

This one is for you, Ethan Cole Johnson. My prayer for you every day is that you will know how much your mother loves you and adores your playful and teasing spirit that I tried so hard to capture within this story.

And the answer to your teasing question after all these years, is still, "No. You were not adopted."

Contents

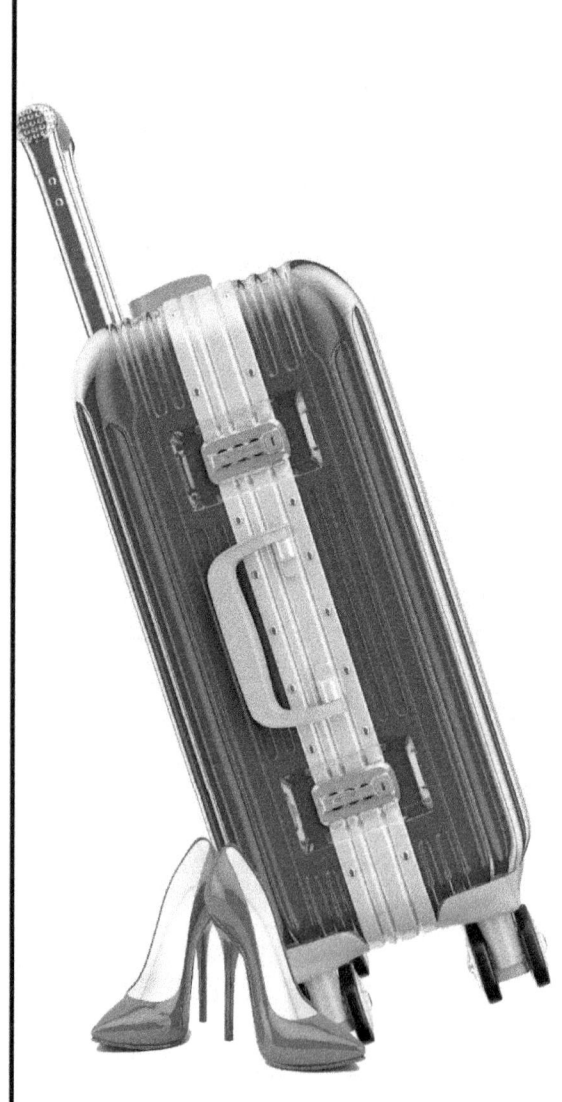

Chapter One

To Expedition or Not to Expedition

Bacon sizzled and popped in the cast iron frying pan, and the kitchen smelled of comfort—comfort food that is. Pollyanna Reagan took a deep breath and smiled as her son, Ethan, and her husband, Marc, entered together.

Life was good, even though it would be changing soon with Ethan going off to college in South Carolina. Their Kentucky home just wouldn't be the same.

"Mom?" Ethan pulled out a chair and sat down.

"Yes." Polly gave him her full attention.

"Would you mind if I begged off on the expedition this weekend? The gang wants me to hang out with them."

Marc had picked up the newspaper she'd left for him by his plate. "Two words I never want to hear in this house, son, are gang and hang out." He slapped the paper against his hand and set it back down.

"That's three words, Dad." Ethan slumped his shoulders. "I guess you're on Mom's side with another boring trip into the woods."

Polly turned her back to the two men in her life and pushed the bacon around the skillet. She flipped a pancake on the griddle.

Pain rose in her like a tsunami wave. Would Marc abandon her, too? She chided herself for the irrational thought and put the pancake on the plate.

Warmth touched her shoulders, and Polly leaned back into another comfort—that of her husband's arms. Marc, busy in his profession as the chief psychiatrist and director at the Jimmy Reagan Children's Behavioral Center didn't show much affection these days, and she craved it from him—needed it in the worst way. Ethan's leaving would create a huge hole in their hearts, and she feared all her years raising her son had left a void in her relationship with her husband.

"Ethan, your mom wants to spend time with you before you head out of town, and as much as she's carted you and your friends all over the place to football games, tennis lessons and matches, and you name it, I think you can show her the respect she deserves."

As soon as Ethan had been born, Polly had left her

lucrative position at a local law firm where she'd been slated to become the next partner. Instead, she'd stayed home to raise her son—something she and Marc had decided upon after the death of Marc's younger brother's son, Jimmy, to a drug overdose. The sacrifice of her job had been well worth it. Ethan had thrived with the attention she was able to shower upon him and the discipline she and Marc had instilled in him.

Ethan remained silent, but her son had a tender heart. What he wanted and what his father shamed him into doing were two different things. He would comply if only for her. She needed to remove the shame from him and give him another reason to join the family—and she had just the right incentive.

She moved the now cooked bacon to a paper towel on a plate and then lifted the pancake to another, which she handed to Marc. "You know, I guess you could forego this trip, but that would mean I have to put up with Aunt Connie in the woods for an entire weekend without you." She poured more batter onto the griddle.

Marc winked at Polly, and she drank up the familiar attraction she'd always had to him. "Connie's agreed to a Bigfoot expedition? Connie of the flashy red high heels who hasn't lived a moment without the convenience of electricity? That Connie?"

"That would be the one I'm talking about." Polly

smiled. Maybe she was looking forward to this weekend beyond the usual anticipation of spending quality time with her husband and her son. Seeing her ever-the-executive sister in the wilds would be too much fun to pass up.

Ethan didn't answer until Polly finished getting the plates to the table and sat down with her family. Then he munched his bacon for a long moment, a slow smile coming to his lips. "Mom, if you can get Aunt Connie to come with us on this expedition, I'll gladly go with you all summer long."

Polly held up her fist. "Deal!"

Ethan bumped it. "This ought to be interesting. When is Aunt Connie coming?"

"She texted me last night." Marc stood and poured himself a cup of coffee. "The luncheon for the presentation of the grant from the Wright Foundation is today at noon. She'll drive here after that."

Polly touched her husband's hand. "Will this grant give you some relief? Will you be able to hire other counselors to free up some time?"

Marc patted her hand. "I hope so, but fentanyl is moving into this part of Appalachia so quickly, I'm sure those resources will be taxed before too long." He pointed to Ethan. "And that's why the words we use in our conversations are important. *Gang* and *hang out* are words that create a mindset, especially for young men your age. *Friends* and *spend time* would be more appropriate. Remember that when you're away from here, will you?"

Ethan nodded and scarfed down his food. "Well, some friends and I are going to spend time working to earn extra cash for college. Gotta go." He kissed Polly's cheek and slapped hands with his father.

He stopped in the doorway. "Mom, I'm sorry that I said the trips are boring."

"Are they?" Polly stood and picked up her dishes.

"Yeah, right. How can they be with people like Reilly, Myrtle, and Fred looking for Old Hairy? I just don't believe in Bigfoot, so we're out there looking for something that doesn't exist."

"Gotcha." Polly nodded. "But you'll humor me, right?"

"Yeah. Well, I do enjoy fishing at Yatesville Lake with Dad and sitting at the dam with you. So, not a total loss. And seeing Aunt Connie in the woods—that's going to be a classic." Ethan ran off.

So, he wasn't just tagging along with her to sit at the dam. He wanted to be there with her. Warmth flamed in Polly's heart.

Marc shared a warm smile with her, and Polly leaned against the counter. She'd enjoy a couple of extra minutes with her husband, but would he brush her away like he often did when she asked him to stay longer?

Marc stood and put his chair under the table.

Polly picked up his dishes. "Do you think it's boring?"

He stopped in the doorway where their son had stood. "No, Polly. I appreciate the fact that you want time away with us, and I find the place relaxing. However," he laughed aloud, "Connie is going to make it anything but peaceful if you manage to get her out there."

Polly placed the dishes in the sink. "Oh, believe me, honey. I will get Connie out in the woods looking for a big beast, and she will go without complaint. These weekends are that important to me."

Chapter Two

You've Got to be Kidding Me

Polly shook out the blanket and let it float down onto the guestroom bed. She was the older sister. Why did spending time with Connie since she'd reached adulthood always cause Polly's nerves to ratchet up to a ten on the Richter scale of emotional seismic activity?

The shutting of a car door drew Polly to the window.

Connie had gotten out of her rental and was pulling an overnight bag from the backseat. Her sister wore her signature red in the form of a flowery shirt over white dress pants. Her jacket, pocketbook, and stilettoes all matched the shade in her shirt.

Polly looked down at her blue jeans, her drab t-shirt, and her too-long-since-replaced tennis shoes. If her husband wasn't a behavioral scientist, she'd declare she hadn't worn these things to set off her sister. The truth was, he was a behavioral scientist, and she had learned some things in her college psych class as well.

Polly took her time getting downstairs. She took a deep breath and opened the door. "You're here."

"And you weren't there," Connie glared. "Didn't Marc ask you to attend the luncheon? I specifically asked that of him?"

Polly stepped back. "I'm glad to see you, too. Come on in. And, no, Marc didn't ask me to come to the center, and I suspect I know his reasons."

"Did he tell you that I requested that you take an active role for the company in our endowment of this and future grants?"

"Connie, I . . ." Polly turned away. This was a hamster wheel upon which she did not want to jump. "Since Marc is to be our messenger, did he tell you our plans for the weekend?"

Connie shook her head. "He's closed mouthed, that one. I had a lot to discuss, but he brushed me off. I'm hoping you'll both be looking over the paperwork I've prepared to make you liaison between the non-profit and the behavioral center while I can be here to answer any questions. Otherwise, I thought we'd have a quiet weekend to visit."

Either Marc had chickened out as messenger

between the sisters, or Connie had wanted to discuss something that Polly should hear. Her husband never liked to discuss details twice or to discuss someone when they weren't present. He'd said enough times that he listened to others talk about loved ones without once having brought any particular problems regarding that person.

And if that wasn't the case and he had chickened out, Polly didn't blame him. He never liked coming between her and any of her family members.

Yet his lack of invite to the luncheon bothered her. Why shouldn't she have been there to celebrate an endowment from her family's non-profit, the Wright Foundation? She had agreed when Connie had presented the possibility of the endowment to be the go-between for the two organizations. That was the least she could do, answer a few questions, keep Connie in the loop, give updates on the endowment to Marc. Nothing taxing at all.

Polly smiled despite concerns that Marc hadn't wanted her to share in the giving of the gift. "We have something more exciting planned for your visit."

"I truly didn't come here for excitement, Pollyanna. I came to work and relax."

"Working and relaxing are only parallel in your universe, not mine. And don't call me Pollyanna, Constance, at least not the way you say it."

"I don't know what you mean?"

"Yes, you do. I'm not a pollyanna in nature simply because I'm satisfied with the life I've chosen."

"So tell me, why are we seeking excitement this weekend if you're satisfied with what you have going on here?"

Polly swallowed hard and bit back the retort. Connie would never understand. She didn't have a family of her own to care for, and Polly doubted her sister ever would. "My son is leaving for college at the end of the summer, and we've been enjoying time together since early spring. I hoped you would join us."

Connie straightened and seemed to relax. "Well, pray tell, just what type of excitement are we getting into this weekend?"

Polly smiled, probably a little too big, but she couldn't help it. "We're going on a Bigfoot expedition."

Connie dropped her overnight bag to the floor. "You're crazy if you think that I'm going out in the wilderness and hunting a make-believe thing. That has all the exhilaration of watching the mold grow on the cheese in my refrigerator."

"Believe it or not, there have been sightings at Yatesville Lake, so your theory that they don't exist is about as valid as mine that they just might. And you are going because your nephew is looking forward to spending time with you in the woods."

Connie half-laughed, half-coughed. "And what makes him think I'd enjoy that time?"

Polly placed her hands on her hips and leaned in to her sister's face. "Because, baby girl, my son wants to spend time with his long-absent aunt, and this is how he wants to spend it."

Connie opened her mouth to speak but clamped it shut.

Polly turned to lead her inside.

"I don't have any clothes," Connie smirked, "or shoes."

"I'll find you some."

"Uh-no." Connie raised her hands as if auctioning off Polly's choice in clothing. "I'll find my own."

"Deal," Polly held out her hand. "I'll let you shop while I get everything packed."

Connie hesitated for a moment and then nodded without taking Polly's hand of truce. "That works for me. But let me get this straight so all our cards are on the table here. "It's really you and not Ethan that wants me on this expedition because I'm actually going to be your weekend entertainment."

"You know me so well, Constance."

Connie finally shook Polly's extended hand. "Anything to make you happy, Pollyanna."

The Visitor Meets Old Hairy

Polly climbed the stairs, and the too big smile on her face grew even larger with each step.

Chapter Three

Bears Are Colorblind, Aren't They?

After three previous expeditions in the same locale, Polly had the setup down pat. Of course, Connie had run them late, though.

Ashland, Kentucky, was no Chicago, as Polly had learned and had coped with for many years, but there were clothing stores that offered high-end casual clothing. Apparently, Connie had found all of them. She'd come home with a multitude of bags from her spree. Polly could only shake her head at the prima donna.

With the tents up and their area made comfortable, Polly sat down in a lawn chair beside her sister.

Connie munched on a bag of chips Ethan had given to her. She dipped her red nails into the bag, brought out a chip, and placed it in her mouth. "Haven't had these in years," she said while eating.

"Reminds me of the time when a snack like that resulted in your face and hair being full of French onion dip." Polly smiled at the memory, turned and brushed her sister's hair from her face. Once upon a time, Connie had looked up to her as a second mama-type but not any longer. Polly pulled her hand away. "Isn't it nice out here? You should take a walk with Ethan. Yatesville Park is a peaceful place to roam."

"A peaceful place with make-believe cryptic manlike apes, you mean." Connie smirked in her sister's direction.

Polly ignored her sister's attempt to tease her. "Make believe or not, they provide a nice time to get away with my family, and as a member of such, I'm glad you decided to come."

"What was it you said when I made a last-ditch effort to stay home: you'd expect the gutters cleaned when you got back." Connie laughed.

Polly had to hand it to her sister. She still had some humor when it came to things outside her box of normal.

A man approached through the clearing. Reilly Jantzen's tent had been set up when they arrived, but he must have left and returned.

"Let me introduce you to the expedition's leader."

Polly patted Connie's chair and stood.

Connie remained sitting, her guarded gaze on Reilly. "Why is he dressed like a rogue archeologist looking for the holy grail?"

"Shh . . . shh." Polly batted at her sister. "He's a character. That's all. They all are. Wait until you meet Myrtle and Fred."

"You mean Ethel and Fred, don't you?" Connie bantered. "And you and yours are Lucy, Ricky, and Ricky, Jr., right?"

Polly stared, her mouth open, feigning surprise. "You actually know something about television that aired before you were born. I'm impressed." She tugged Connie with her to approach the man.

"Where are the boys?" Reilly asked while at the same time looking Connie over as if she were a life-size steak kabob.

"They went fishing. Should be back here any minute." Polly tucked her sister a little behind her. Some habits were hard to break, but Reilly had never looked at Polly in that way. If he had, Marc would have decked him, she was sure. "Reilly Jantzen, I'd like you to meet my sister, Connie Wright. She's visiting with us this weekend, and we thought she'd enjoy the expedition."

Reilly wore a pair of brown pants over a white shirt dotted with dirt stains. The man had been working at something. A brimmed hat with a black band sat on his sandy blond head of hair. He smiled a crooked smile. "That's why you paid extra. I wasn't sure."

"I told you in the e-mail." Polly sighed. Did men ever read anything a woman wrote, even correspondence about business?

"You paid for this?" Connie chortled. "And you had to set up the tent."

"Reilly rents the area for the weekend, Connie." Polly shook her head.

"And I buy the steaks and such." Reilly narrowed his eyes in Connie's direction. "You'll thank me later." He waved his hand up and down the length of Connie's outfit, a bright red pair of shorts with a red striped top. "That what you're wearing? Good thing we're hunting for Old Hairy in the dark. The bears would sure be interested in you. But, hey, maybe Old Hairy will be intrigued, too."

Connie smirked and gave a small shake of her head. "A lot you know. Animals are color-blind."

Reilly leaned in. "Are they?"

Connie backed away. "Why do they call him Old Hairy?"

"'Cuz he's old and hairy," Reilly laughed. "People started seeing him, and we started calling him that."

Polly looked over Connie's head. "Here come Fred

and Myrtle. I'll help them set up their tent."

Connie picked up the bag of chips from her chair and reseated herself.

Reilly rubbed his stubbled chin and uttered some sound that may have been laughter or just a sputter in Connie's direction. Then he moved around Polly and greeted the Conrads.

Connie stood. "I'm sorry I didn't help you earlier, but I was starving. I should have stopped and gotten something besides coffee when I was shopping. But I really do need to speak with you, sis. About some plans I have for your involvement as a legal liaison for the foundation and the behavioral center."

Legal liaison. That was more than Polly had contemplated, more than she wanted to take on, actually. "Let's shelf that conversation for later. We're not in the board room, you know." She moved to greet the newcomers and glanced back at her sister.

"Myrtle, it's good to see you." Polly stepped toward the older woman who had become such a treasure to her over the past few months and held out her hand to take some of the bags Myrtle toted with her.

Myrtle was all of five feet, and she was a thin little thing, always in motion. Her tightly curled hair was kept short, and despite her age, which Polly assumed was inching into the mid-seventies, her blue eyes were clear and hawklike.

Fred on the other hand was a giant of a man. Though only approaching six feet, his girth was stout, and an older knee injury caused him to hobble a little when they hiked. Marc usually kept close to him in case he fell and needed help getting up. So far, that had not occurred.

Fred seemed to enjoy the time around the camp, and he'd explained that the antique tent they used was from their early days of camping. The thing didn't have a floor. Myrtle would spread out thick blankets. Anyone or anything could get under the sides of the old covering, but they insisted they were fine and used to it.

Polly took the two bags Myrtle handed her, and when Fred located the perfect spot for their tent, she placed them on the ground.

Myrtle wrapped her in her arms. "Good to see you, my girl."

"Likewise." Polly stepped back and right into her sister. "Sorry," she muttered. "Myrtle, I'd like you to meet the baby of my family, Connie Wright, who has agreed to join our expedition this month. She's actually somewhat of a family sleuth, so she might come across something to help us find Old Hairy."

Connie sputtered and held out her hand. "Nice to meet you, Myrtle." She turned to Fred. "You, too, Fred."

"Likewise." Fred held out his hand.

"Well, Fred, let's get that tent up, shall we?" Connie took command.

Polly smiled and relaxed. Maybe her sister was getting into the expedition after all.

The Visitor Meets Old Hairy

Chapter Four

Do You See What I See?

For about the fifth time, Polly had to turn to her sister with her finger to her lips.

In the darkness, it was a little hard to see, but slowly, Polly's eyes were becoming accustomed to her surroundings.

"I'm not talking." Connie's attempt to whisper had the decibels of a seven-forty-seven. "I'm walking here." Wind whipped hair into her face. "And who can hear anything with this wind." She swirled her hands above her head to indicate the swishing leaves. "Give us a little rain, and we'll have a hurricane."

"Try not to step on the twigs." Polly ignored her sister's complaints.

"We're not on a path, Polly. The ground is littered

with them."

Ethan's snicker took the air of frustration from Polly's wings. She leaned against a tree and covered her face with her hands, trying to keep from bursting into laughter.

Connie leaned against her, her body shaking. "And if Old Hairy was out here, we most definitely would see him."

"No." Ethan came near. "Aunt Connie, you're not up on your Bigfoot information. They're stealthy. They are hard to spot even in the daytime. They can hide themselves against the trees and not make a sound unless they want to be heard or seen—all eight feet—no grunting from exertion, no stomping when they walk." He glanced at his mom with a sly smile that barely showed in the moonlight. "Some people even believe they have a cloaking ability like one of those lizards in Florida that change colors."

Marc drew near. "And they can read your mind." He wiggled his brows and glanced at his wife. "When they're near you, their sub-sonic hum can make you deathly ill."

They were making fun of her, but Polly didn't care. Standing alone with her family in the middle of their expedition area and gabbing with the people she loved, that was all she wanted. "They hide in caves and traverse that way. That's why they aren't seen," she countered with her own knowledge of Bigfoot lore. "And they've had years to adapt to the land, and they know the layout."

"There are no caves in this park." Ethan swatted at a mosquito that by some show of strength moved against the wind.

They remained silent for a moment as the limbs above them rustled.

"Did you hear that?" Connie spun around.

"With the wind?" Polly threw her sister's words back at her.

Connie waved her hands back and forth in front of her face. "And smell that?"

Polly took a deep breath and coughed. "That's not a Bigfoot." The wind must have brought the odor to them.

"It's a skunk." Ethan took off running through the dark in the direction of the camp.

Connie put her hands out to stop Marc and Polly. "Let's see if he runs into it first."

Marc laughed aloud. "Good idea."

Polly spied something illuminated by the rays of the moon filtering through the trees: the white of a skunk's coat.

Perhaps Ethan had been the clever one.

Polly held to her sister's and her husband's arms. "There." She nodded.

The skunk stood up on two feet and looked around.

Polly held her breath, and not from the stench. Did skunks attack?

The skunk stayed still for a moment, looked behind it, and then turned to look in their direction.

Polly planted her feet so as to run if it moved toward her.

"Did it widen its eyes?" Marc joked.

Despite the wind, tromping on the grass could be heard and then came a heavy grunt.

The skunk took off.

Connie—and Marc—jumped behind Polly's back.

More stomping sounded, coming closer.

An overly large figure silhouetted in the moon's shine moved into the center of the trees. His attention was in the direction the skunk had fled.

Connie gasped.

The creature stilled completely. Then it turned.

"Don't move." Marc's whisper was a command. "Polly, is it a man?"

"I-I don't think so." She trembled. "He's huge."

The huge ape-like man stared. When it blinked, the action was slow.

It swayed back and forth like an ape.

"We're about to find out if it's color blind." Polly reached for her sister's hand.

Connie held on to her. "Not funny, Pollyanna."

"Wasn't trying to be." Polly took a step back, forcing Marc and Connie to come with her.

The creature blinked again. Then it raised its shoulders, bent low at the knees, and inhaled. As it stood again, a tremendous howl built from its innards and reverberated against Polly. She'd never heard anything the likes of it.

The howl ended, and the creature stood stock-still, his attention never leaving them.

"Shoo. Shoo." Connie moved her free hand.

The lumbering beast stared at Connie, blinked again, and turned. Then it thundered off into the woods.

Polly released her breath. "Was it really . . .?"

Connie stood, hands on hips. "No, it wasn't. I can guarantee you that it was that ridiculous Reilly Jantzen. He's donned a hunter's ghillie suit."

"I don't, for one minute, believe that was a Bigfoot, but that wasn't a ghillie suit," Marc corrected. "That costume was made and made well."

"Whatever it was . . ." Connie sighed. ". . . that Reilly wants you to believe it was a Bigfoot so that, in the least, you'll come back for another expedition. And if he's fortunate, you'll spread the word and give him the advertisement he needs to make a boatload of money."

"But that sound. That wasn't a man." Polly nearly

stumbled.

He could have a wireless microphone in that suit," Connie countered.

Marc gave a half-laugh. "Yeah, maybe. But whoever that was seemed much larger than Reilly."

"Or any man," Polly agreed.

Connie shrugged. "Put on some elevated shoes, throw on a few coats, and there you have it. Reilly Jantzen drumming up business from the gullible."

"Gee, thanks." Polly shoulder-butted her sister.

"I think I've had enough excitement for the night." Connie moved through the brush, making almost as much noise as the creature—or man—or whatever it was.

Polly caught up and tugged her to stop. "How can you be so sure it wasn't Old Hairy?"

Connie shrugged. "Come on, Polly. This is up there with aliens. You have to admit. It's rather hard to believe."

"Locals have seen him before." She held out her hand toward the clearing where the whatever-it-was had been. "And after . . . that?"

"Ask yourself one question." Connie tilted her head toward her sister.

"What's that?" Marc asked.

She gestured in the direction the skunk had skedaddled. "What self-respecting man-ape would tangle with Pepe Le Pew? And I thought they smelled worse than a skunk. I didn't smell anything different from him."

"I was too afraid to smell," Polly admitted.

Marc laughed and wrapped Polly in an embrace. "Your sister may be on to something. Let's go back to camp and see how long it takes Reilly to get back there."

They tramped through the woods, no longer trying to be silent and ten minutes later emerged at camp.

Reilly, Myrtle, Fred, and Ethan were sitting around a fire, roasting marshmallows.

"Look who beat us back," Ethan announced. "I found these three lazing around. Had to ask if they'd even left camp. Here they were, campfire blazing, marshmallows roasting. Yum."

Polly turned to look at her sister. "Next theory, Sherlock."

The Visitor Meets Old Hairy

Chapter Five

Bigfoot Hunting Is Murder

Polly lay awake. Someone had been moving around in the camp, but the sound had gone silent. In fact, everything had gone quiet including the wind.

One of the other campers had probably needed to seek the privacy of the wooded area beyond the tents. Polly had rolled over and closed her eyes. But the eerie stillness clamored for her attention. Nothing. Not one cricket or nocturnal bird. No coyote howls. Nothing scampered in the brush nearby.

Connie rolled over and smacked Polly in the face.

Her son was sleeping with his never-move-between-midnight-and-dawn father, and Polly had whack-a-mole Connie beside her.

Smack!

"Connie!" Polly bolted upright, ending the nocturnal silence around her.

Connie didn't move.

Polly scooted closer to the tent edge and out of the arm-shot of her sister.

A thud hit the earth beside the tent, sending Polly skittering back toward Connie. Another thud sent reverberation through the ground.

"Connie." Polly tugged.

Connie remained still.

A low grunt and another thump beside the tent lifted the hairs on Polly's arms. She couldn't breathe as she lay there listening. Someone had paused outside the tent flap. Were they planning on coming inside? The moon must have been behind a cloud because not one shadow was cast against the tent's cloth.

Whoever it was took a deep breath, grunted, and walked away.

Polly inhaled deeply and sat up. She stared at her sleeping sister. The family said she was a master amateur sleuth—a clear oxymoron—not that she displayed any of that ability at the moment.

Connie inhaled with a snore and threw her arm in the other direction.

Polly climbed onto her haunches and slowly unzipped the tent flap. She looked right and then left, even up, before she climbed outside.

Her bladder was telling her she needed the privacy of the woods now, but her feet and her head said she'd stand right there and mess her pants rather than go into those woods alone.

She bent down to look into the tent. "Connie!" she spat a decibel barely under a whisper. "Connie, wake up!"

Her sister didn't move.

Polly raised up and stretched. "Time to take off the big gal—" No. She wouldn't say it. Too obvious. She stepped toward the tree line.

A loud bellow hit the air from somewhere out in the woods—the same call they'd heard earlier supposedly from Old Hairy—yet the others at the campfire had claimed the sound had not reached them. Connie had surmised that the wind had buffered the terrifying noise, but Polly's sister had not come up with another explanation to explain the fact Reilly had been at camp.

Behind Polly, Connie climbed from the tent. "That sounded like someone was being murdered."

Polly put on her brave face and crossed her legs. "Don't be silly. It was a coyote kill or something like that."

Again, everything in the woods had fallen silent.

"They say it can be deafening, don't they?" Connie

asked.

"What?"

"Silence."

Polly listened to the eerie quietness again and then shook her head. "I need to go to the bathroom."

"Are you kidding?" Connie half-laughed. "That designated area is a stretch out there. Pee in a cup or something."

Polly giggled. "Dad used to pull that one on us with car trips. Did it ever work for him?" She stepped back inside the tent and pulled her shoes on. Then she scooped up Connie's red sneakers and held them out to her. "Come with?"

Connie stepped inside and pulled them on.

It would be a little easier to have her sister with her. Polly opened the flap and then halted when a figure stood in front of her.

"Sorry." Myrtle backed up. "I was heading to the privy."

"Seems we had the same idea." Polly leaned back into the tent. "Myrtle and I can go if you want to go back to sleep."

Connie climbed from the tent. "You got me thinking I need to go. Three of us are safer than two alone."

"You afraid?" Myrtle smiled. "There's nothing out here that will hurt us. Nothing in the world." The conviction rang from the older woman like a church bell, as if she had to convince herself of that truth.

"So . . ." Connie sighed. "You don't believe Bigfoot is stomping around Yatesville Lake?"

Myrtle blinked and seemed startled by the question. "What makes you think that? Why would I be out here in the dead of night? Didn't you say you heard him?"

Polly placed her hand on Myrtle's shoulder. "I think she was commenting on your statement that there's nothing to be afraid of out here. You seem pretty adamant about that, but I would think Old Hairy would be dangerous." The one they'd seen sure seemed as if he could take them apart without effort. Yet the big fellow's only threatening gesture had been his howl.

Myrtle waved her hands as if the statement was a ridiculous one. "Fiddlesticks. Those creatures are wise. Why do you think they're so hard to find?"

"Well, according to Polly, what we saw in the woods was a Bigfoot."

The words Connie spoke registered a second too late for Polly to react. They had only mentioned the howl. The sighting of the creature had remained their secret. Ethan didn't even know.

"You saw what?" Myrtle practically did a Yosemite Sam hop. "Where? When?"

Polly widened her eyes at her little sister, not sure

Connie hadn't spilled the beans on purpose. As the youngest child, Connie had often tipped over a can of legumes in order to share something with her parents that her older siblings had not wanted told. Even as fully grown adults, they were often in awkward positions with Mom and Dad due to the baby with big ears and a mouth to match.

Connie shrugged. "Either he's out there or he's not. If you really believe in him, Polly, why wouldn't you tell the others? Isn't that why you're here?"

Just like when Connie was a schoolgirl.

Polly started to offer an excuse, but Connie had her dead to rights. She did not know why Marc remained silent about their earlier sighting, but Polly had kept the secret because she couldn't grasp the truth of what she'd seen out there in the woods—where a particular bush sat that was calling her name. "Look, I really am reaching urgent capacity here. Can we argue about this from behind different trees?"

Connie giggled.

Myrtle didn't ask any other questions, but she stared off into the darkness. Then, as if having an afterthought, she held up her finger in a silent plea for them to wait for her.

She dipped down and seemed to rummage in her tent. Then she straightened, paused for a moment, shook her head, and backed out carrying a roll of toilet paper and a flashlight. "When in the woods, these are a girl's best friends."

Myrtle's humor, though, did not match the pale of her wrinkled face when she turned on the lantern's beam. Had the discussion about Old Hairy scared her, or was there something else on her mind?

Connie left Polly no time to truly ponder the question. She trudged forward on the path.

"You saw him, huh?" Myrtle whispered as they walked.

"The reason I didn't say anything is because I'm still trying to fathom it," Polly confessed. "We thought it might have been Reilly, but he couldn't have gotten out of a ghillie suit or a costume and back to the camp. And it seems he was already there when we saw the creature."

Myrtle stopped and narrowed her eyes, and her face went hard as granite. Then she shook her head. "No. Reilly was with me and Fred the entire time you were gone. We'd been in the woods with Reilly and arrived back at camp ten minutes before Ethan returned without the three of you."

"But you think he's capable of doing something like that, don't you?"

Myrtle half-laughed and continued the trek beside Polly. "Darling, Reilly's not all that he seems. And I suspect he's not all that fond of running into Bigfoot."

"But he has," Polly sputtered. "It's why we're out here, right? He saw it and wants to see it again."

"Yes, he saw her as big as life, and no. He doesn't want to see her again."

"Her?" Polly nearly stumbled, except for the solid force she hit.

Polly crashed into Connie, and Myrtle tripped over Polly's feet.

Polly grasped Myrtle's arm to keep the older woman from falling. "Connie! Watch what you're doing?"

Connie didn't speak. Her finger was on her lips, but not in a silencing motion. Polly knew that look. Connie was contemplating.

Polly looked around her sister.

And gasped.

Beside her, Myrtle went white. Her body slacked, and Polly was glad she hadn't let go.

A man lay face up in a heap on the ground. His clothes were disheveled with dirt blotches all over them. His rifle lay some feet away from him, and his eyes were wide with a terror that he could obviously no longer feel. Blood dripped from a heavy gash in his forehead.

Myrtle seemed to gain strength. She stepped forward. "Do you think Old Hairy killed Reilly Jantzen?"

Chapter Six

A Large and Hairy Suspect

The Kentucky State Police arrived in strength within the hour. Crime scene investigators combed the area beyond the campsite on and around the wooded path where Reilly Jantzen's body lay roped off by yellow tape.

Near the tents, Polly had been separated from Connie and Myrtle, and all three were kept at a distance to keep them from overhearing the questions fired at each of them by the officers conducting the on-scene interrogations.

Polly tried to look around the detective, who said her name was Lantana—Polly wasn't sure if that was her first name or her last. The rather tall and big-boned woman had ample cleavage that stretched her suit buttons. Her blond, bouffant hairdo took her to nearly six and a half feet and could have vied easily with the most popular female country stars of the 60s and 70s. Whether purposeful or not, Lantana moved when Polly moved, thus keeping Polly from seeing her husband and son.

"You say that you heard someone outside your tent approximately ten minutes before you and your friends found the body." Lantana continued her interrogation.

"I heard something. I assume it was a human being."

The woman's lips tilted in a sarcastic direction. "What'd you think it was, Bigfoot?"

Warmth traveled up Polly's neck and into her face.

"Don't tell me that's exactly what you think?" The detective stepped in, as if daring Polly to share that she would be an unreliable witness.

"No." Polly returned the smirk. "Seriously, you must believe in Bigfoot to even suggest such a thing."

The woman shifted her weight and looked out into the woods, almost as if looking over her shoulder. "No. No. Can't say I do. What did you mean?"

"Some larger creature or a human was outside the tent. I didn't get up and look." Polly caught a glimpse of Ethan hanging out around the edges of the make-do interrogation spots. The nosy boy was listening in, she was sure.

"What brought you three ladies out then?"

"We needed to use the bathroom."

Lantana nodded and looked to her companions who had almost simultaneously stepped away from Connie and Myrtle. Maybe their preliminary interrogations were a game of twenty questions. Polly hadn't counted, but that seemed to be the number.

"One last question," Lantana promised.

Okay twenty-one.

"What in the world were you folks doing out here with a known criminal like Reilly Jantzen?"

Polly widened her eyes. "Known criminal? He wasn't known to me. I mean I know him. My family and I've camped out here with him before, but I live in Ashland. We've been meeting up and camping out here for a weekend each month. Reilly was the expedition leader."

Lantana squinted her eyes. "Expedition?"

Polly's eyelids hurt as they widened again. She'd have to admit to this detective that they were on a hunt for an elusive hairy creature. Polly and her family would be laughingstocks. Marc would have to prove that he was sane enough to head a children's behavioral center even if he was the force behind it. What had she done?

"So, were you folks out here helping him find something?"

"We were—"

"Did he tell you about the money he hid? Is it true that he lost it?"

If Polly's eyes widened any further, they'd flap over her forehead and swallow up the back of her head. "Money? No. He never said anything about money. What are you talking about?"

"We found a shovel in the woods. There's a hole there as well. A deep one. Are you sure you didn't kill the man and hide the money?"

Polly laughed aloud. "That's almost as ridiculous as Bigfoot running loose in the camp." She clamped her mirthful lips together.

Lantana leaned closer. "So, tell me. What were you searching for on this so-called expedition?"

"Detective Frasier," a uniformed officer called to her. "We have something over here that you have to see."

Detective Lantana Frasier held up her hand in a demand for the young man to remain silent. "Mrs. Reagan, what is it you and your family met up with Reilly Jantzen to explore if it wasn't the money?"

Connie trounced forward. "Tell her, Polly. Better she know the truth than to think you were cavorting with a bank robber."

Lantana closed her eyes slowly and opened them at double-slow speed. She released a sigh. "Don't tell me you all were out here doing . . ."

Thank goodness for her forehead. Polly was sure her eyelids would have wrapped around her head and down to her feet. "Detective! My son is here. Shame on you."

The detective shook her head. "I was going to say doing the family thing with a group of new friends."

"They were doing the family thing," Connie broached. "With a twist."

"Ho, now." Lantana straightened. "Ain't you her sister?"

"Polly has her family out here hunting for Bigfoot. I'm assuming the expedition gave Reilly Jantzen the cover he needed to look for his money." Connie placed her hands on her hips. "I got dragged out here this weekend."

Lantana stared at Polly, and then she smiled. "So, you still want to tell me you didn't think Bigfoot was wandering around your camp tonight?"

"Bigfoot was not wandering around our camp tonight."

Myrtle entered the circle. "But he was out here earlier. Polly and Connie saw him."

Lantana now seemed to have trouble keeping her eyelids from doing a flip. "You saw a Bigfoot?" She looked from Connie to Polly.

Connie shook her head. "We saw an unidentified large being in the woods. And since we do not believe in

Bigfoot, we do not believe the creature was a Bigfoot."

Lantana slapped her book shut and leaned in toward the three women. "Just don't you be so sure about that, you hear?" She walked away.

For an all-business executive, there were times when Connie still had that little-sister-big-mouth thing going on. This time, she'd put them all in trouble. Polly's hand—yes, her hand—because she'd never hit another human being in her life, reached out to smack her little sister upside the head, but she didn't. At the last minute, she rolled her fingers into a fist and pulled her hand back to her chest. She needed the comfort of her husband's embrace. Marc wasn't in sight. Neither was Ethan.

A large contingency of officers returned to camp from the woods. In their midst were her husband and her son and Detective Frasier.

Ethan ran toward her, his eyes bright and his face awash in wonder as if he were twelve and not going to be eighteen. "Mom! Mom! They're casting footprints, Old Hairy's prints. They lead right to his nest. You gotta see it. I heard 'em say that if they aren't real, you ladies have a lot of explaining to do."

"Aren't real? And what nest? Do Bigfoot make nests—like birds?" Connie snorted. "They aren't real, Ethan. And what do they have to do with us?"

"No matter." The detective pointed from Polly to

Connie and back again. "You'll stay here in Lawrence County until you are told that you can leave."

"Wait a minute." Connie straightened to her full height, but Lantana still had several inches on her below the bouffant. "I am heading home to Chicago in another couple of days. I already have my flight."

Lantana gave a mirthless smile. "No, you're staying here where I can keep an eye on you."

"At least let us go back to Ashland." Nothing in Polly really wanted to stay here at this point. "It's only in the next county."

"You're staying here." Lantana glared at her.

She couldn't possibly disapprove. "There's a state police headquarters there, for pity's sake."

"And it's not here." Lantana lifted her eyebrows. "No."

"This is ridiculous." Polly hadn't said it very loudly, but apparently, it had been noisy enough.

Lantana Frasier made her way toward her. "There's a dead man in one direction, killed from blunt-force trauma to his head, a hole that clearly held a container large enough to store money in another direction, several large, and not really human, footprints, and they all lead from one place—a tree structure. Either someone's framing Bigfoot for Reilly Jantzen's murder or Bigfoot did the dirty deed and got away a rich man."

She strolled past but turned, looking Polly dead in the eyes. "Or there's the scenario I like best: Bigfoot did kill Reilly Jantzen, and he's framing it on y'all."

Chapter Seven

A Little Room for Skepticism

Polly couldn't get close enough to Marc as they stood staring at the elaborate structure roped off by crime scene tape. One would think the murder occurred at this monstrous configuration of limbs—no, not limbs—actual trees. The trees had been leaned together at the top to form a teepee-like abode. Either the structure had not been there during their previous two expeditions, or they had never ventured this far from the campsite.

One thing for sure: this configuration was not made by a mere man, not without machines. The larger trees could not have been lifted into place by hand. And there was no indication that any equipment had been through here—ever.

They'd stayed after the authorities had abandoned

the scene. Then Marc sent Connie and Ethan off in the only vehicle they had to secure motel rooms in Louisa, the nearest town since they had to stay in the county.

"Someone built it." Marc rubbed the morning stubble on his face and yawned. "Look at the trees and limbs used as walls. They're huge, impossible for a man to move without equipment. Some are fashioned. I don't think a man could bend them, and the area inside is big enough for a very large human." He moved away from her.

Polly was having none of that. She grabbed his arm, tucked hers inside his, and nearly climbed on his back. "Why are we out here?"

Marc tried to escape.

Polly held tight.

He stood and brushed off her hold. "There's nothing to be afraid of."

Polly remembered a time when Marc would have held her close and told her that he always wanted her to need him like this.

She stepped away and put her hands behind her back. "But why couldn't we go with Connie and Ethan?"

"Because I have some questions for you, and I wanted to ask them in private." He leaned against a dogwood tree.

"What? Do you think I killed Reilly?"

He shook his head. "Not in a million years, baby."

That one endearment sent hope into Polly's veins. "Then what?"

"How are you holding up? Besides the fear, I mean."

"Fear is about the only thing that's keeping me going. Someone—or something—killed Reilly Jantzen, and I don't want it coming after us."

"It? Other than that's the name for a murderous clown, it also depersonalizes the killer. You can't believe Old Hairy did this. Do you?"

"You sound like Connie. Isn't there any room for a little belief in your heart? What did we see yesterday?" She waved her hands and stepped away, landed her eyes on the structure, and hurried back closer to her husband. Still, her hands moved in the air. "You just gave a precise rundown of your thoughts on this nest. What built it? What did we see yesterday?"

"A Bigfoot wouldn't dig up a box. Let's put the structure and the sighting aside because those are things I'd like to get to the bottom of, but better people before us haven't been able to solve that mystery. Reilly was killed by a human being for a box. I have no doubt about that."

"Makes sense."

"But as far as we know, there were only seven of us

in the woods. You and I know that we're innocent." He cocked an eyebrow. "Right?" That smile she loved so much radiated his handsome face.

"Right. But while I will never doubt the innocence of my son, I didn't see you."

He pushed away from the tree and kissed her cheek. "That innocent son, the one I'm sure you will say never lies, will vouch for me. Oh, and by the way, he did lie to us last month when we went out of town."

"Oh." Polly tapped her foot. "And what did he lie about?"

"The neighbors asked me if we'd sanctioned a party while we were gone."

"He wouldn't!"

Marc laughed. "He did. But I have it on good authority that the neighbors told him they were watching, and it was a G-rated gig."

Polly laughed. "I really thought I'd taught him about responsibility. The house was so clean when we arrived home that I should have known something was up."

"Anyway, our perfect child will vouch for me. We'll not let the coppers know he has a shady past."

Polly turned to take in the structure. "Other than the two of you, there's one person I can't place."

"Fred." Marc nodded. "So, you see, there is a human component in all of this, a lead to follow.

"But Fred. He's—he's so Fred. Huge, you know. Lumbering because of the knee injury. Couldn't get through the woods quietly," Polly mused.

Fred would huff and puff and sound like a large creature outside of her tent, though. And Myrtle had been startled by something when she looked inside their tent. What if it wasn't something that alarmed her but the lack of something. Or rather, the lack of someone?

Polly turned to give Marc her full attention. "When we found Reilly Jantzen, Myrtle couldn't see him at first, and she was fearful. I'm sure of it. Maybe she thought Fred was laying there."

"Okay. I don't want us to jump to conclusions. I simply wanted you to be aware that Old Hairy isn't the only suspect. I don't believe for a second that some ape-man killed a person for money."

Polly hated that she smiled. After all, a man had died, but she couldn't help it. "What if Reilly dug up the box on his own, and Bigfoot was watching. Something like that would be a bauble to him, don't you think? That chest may never be found if Old Hairy carried it off into the woods." She couldn't resist teasing him.

"Polly . . ."

The snap of tree limbs brought Polly around. She fell against her husband, burrowing into his side.

"Mom!" Ethan broke through the tree line.

"They've made an arrest for the murder. Two of them, actually."

"Ethan Reagan, I asked you to hold up!" Connie's red shirt came into view before she did.

"I wanted to be the one to tell them."

"What do you think?" Connie neared.

"Well, obviously, you two weren't arrested." Marc snatched at Ethan and drew him close. "Who was?"

"Myrtle and Fred," Ethan declared. "That woman detective doubled backed to tell us. The police found the empty cash box in their garage. They probably killed Reilly, took the box, and stashed it away, picking it up and taking it home after the coast was clear."

Connie shook her head. "Those dear people did not kill that man."

Polly wanted to agree, but she and Marc had only just crossed this bridge. They could have. "If they didn't, that leaves us with one suspect." Marc quipped, vocalizing Polly's thoughts. "And I don't think you'll peg it on him either."

"Old Hairy. You bet I am," Connie declared. "Whoever was in that costume killed Reilly Jantzen. I'm sure, and I'm going to prove it. Are you three with me?"

Marc held up his hands. "If you can wrap this investigation up by tomorrow evening, I'm in."

Connie smiled. "I've solved 'em quicker than that

before."

Polly liked to explore, and she liked to walk, so that's what she did, taking a walk from the downtown Louisa, Kentucky, motel before anyone in her family awoke Sunday morning. She'd driven through Louisa before, but walking let her experience the quaint atmosphere. There wasn't much in the way of commerce. The town did have a grocery store or two. Dee's Drive-Inn sat in the middle of town, and the motel manager had indicated it was a good place to eat.

But Louisa had one unique characteristic on which Polly stood and watched the fog drift by. The town bordered West Virginia, and to get to the sister state, one only had to cross a bridge—the only U.S. bridge that traversed two rivers. And if that wasn't enough for visitors to marvel at, the bridge was a T-bridge. A right turn off the bridge would not plunge anyone into the water but would drive them toward a spit of land in which some homes sat, on what the locals in Louisa called The Point.

Polly strode past that turn and back into town, passing Dee's Drive Inn. What was the other place the motel manager had suggested? Oh, yes, Down Home

Grill. The best breakfast money could buy apparently. Marc had promised Ethan they'd get a hearty breakfast before they began their sleuthing with Connie, who claimed to have dug up some information at the local library.

Perhaps she'd let the family in on the scoop over breakfast.

"Excuse me." A man walked toward her.

Polly turned to see if he addressed someone besides her, but she had been the only early morning pedestrian.

"Excuse me," he repeated.

The guy was as round in the middle as he was tall, and he was tall. His feet flopped in front of him, and Polly had to bite her cheek when she envisioned him in a clown suit, makeup covering his face and bald crown. "Yes?"

"I was told that you were at Yatesville Lake when Reilly Jantzen was killed."

Polly didn't know why, but the hairs on her arms stood at attention. She hadn't spoken with anyone about the murder or her vicinity to it. Connie had only done online and library research yesterday afternoon. How could this man pinpoint her?

"I'm a friend of Fred and Myrtle Conrad." He held out his hand. "James Bastien."

Polly hesitated.

"I was with Myrtle and Fred yesterday before they

were arrested. Myrtle told me you were there with her when you all discovered Reilly."

Something wasn't adding up, though, but Polly couldn't put her pointy little finger on it. Had he followed her onto the bridge, and wasn't that something that had a creep factor of one hundred attached to it?

"Myrtle worked for me at the bank. Naturally, she called me when the authorities found the money box in her home." He shifted the weight from one foot to the other "I don't, for one minute, believe that Myrtle was involved in that robbery with Jantzen. She said it was Jantzen back when it happened. She's maintained that all along."

Wait, Myrtle knew about the robbery? She knew Jantzen before they began their Bigfoot expeditions? Myrtle talked about nature and her research of Bigfoot, but nothing really about their personal lives. And she and Fred had only been on the politest of terms with Reilly.

"I don't know anything about the robbery or the trial. I had no idea that Myrtle knew Jantzen or what she did before her retirement."

"Myrtle wanted me to ask if you knew anything that could help her and Fred. Jantzen was acquitted of the robbery, and the Conrads and Jantzen were on friendly terms."

Myrtle and Fred were friends with Jantzen?

Bastien's story wasn't adding up. Polly shook her head. "Detective Lantana—I mean Frasier—said he was a career criminal. Why would the Conrads befriend him?"

Bastien nodded enthusiastically. "Reilly had a previous record: forgery, fraud, anything to turn a quick buck. And believe me. We have no room to doubt that he robbed us that day."

"Did you identify him as the robber?"

"Jantzen wore a mask, but I identified him by his voice and Myrtle agreed. Doesn't matter how we know, but we now know without a doubt that Reilly committed the robbery. If he'd been tried here, he'd have done time, but it was a federal crime, and those are heard elsewhere. Reilly was tried in Ashland, and no one knew him there. Some motion was filed to keep out his criminal history, so Reilly walked, kept the money, and all." As he spoke, a smile began to form.

The creep factor was growing. "You seem awfully pleased that he did."

Bastien blinked. "No, ma'am. I'm not happy that he stole the money. I'm happy that I know he stole the money."

The guy's train of thought had derailed. He wasn't normal. Polly stepped back.

Bastien must have noticed. He tilted his head. "I'm sorry. I'm not making much sense, but I assure you, Mrs.

Reagan, I don't want to see Myrtle and Fred do time for a murder they didn't commit. If you could relay anything you saw in those woods, it would really help me."

"Help you how?" Polly moved around Bastien.

As Bastien moved, he huffed with each step.

"Mr. Bastien, I know nothing more than I told Detective Frasier, and that isn't much." She backed away from him.

Bastien moved forward. "Are you sure? You see, Myrtle was involved."

Polly startled. "In what? She was involved in the robbery?"

"No." Bastien waved his hands as if to erase his words. "She joined in on this expedition nonsense to help Reilly."

"You're not making sense, Mr. Bastien." Polly rubbed her forehead. "And you're not helping Myrtle's case either."

Bastien was making Myrtle out to be an accessory to the crime at least and an accomplice at the most. "I'm sorry. I can't help you." Questions ping-ponged in Polly's brain, but she wasn't about to ask them of this man. Something about him rang false. Frighteningly so.

Bastien seemed sincere, but Polly prided herself on having a good intuition about people. Myrtle didn't strike her as an accomplice to anything beyond maybe the last gardening event.

Bastien could be very well what he seemed: a worried employer with a retired worker charged with a murder she didn't commit, or there could be something else the man was hiding.

Chapter Eight

Everywhere that Connie Went

Polly chomped on her bacon and attempted to ignore her sister once again.

Connie chewed on each attempt she made to produce new information for her adoring fans—her family sitting around the table at Down Home Grill. And she milked every morsel. "As I was saying, Myrtle—"

"Myrtle worked at the bank that Jantzen robbed." Polly pushed the last bite of bacon into her mouth.

Marc and Ethan swiveled their heads as if watching a tennis match.

"For goodness' sake, Polly. Did you read my notes?" Connie sat down her coffee cup.

Polly smiled. "No. And I'm sorry for stealing your thunder, but if you hadn't been so mysterious in order to make us wait for what you dug up, you could have had the scoop."

Connie stabbed her scrambled eggs. "That's not what I was doing. I was thinking it through. I received some information from the Big Sandy News and the other area papers, but the librarian filled me in on some of the other details. I wanted to make sure they jived."

"I think you owe her an apology." Marc elbowed Polly.

"Yes, I agree, and I do apologize. My source came from Myrtle's ex-employer, James Bastien, the manager at the bank. He found me in town this morning. His story was that Myrtle is hoping I saw something that will help her and Fred."

"James Bastien," Connie said the name as if giving it a great deal of thought. "He might be our best avenue for inside information about the robbery. Unless we're to believe Bigfoot killed him for the loot, there had to be someone else who knew Reilly planted the money in the woods."

"An accomplice?" Ethan leaned forward, elbows on the table.

Polly caught his attention and then looked to the offending appendages until he slipped them off the table. Then she continued, "But here's the thing. He told me that Myrtle and Fred were helping Reilly."

Ethan sat back with his arms crossed over his chest, his thumbs hitched in his arm pits for dramatic effect. He knew better than give her a snarky look, especially under Marc's watchful eyes.

Connie eyed Polly and Ethan for a moment. "We'll add Mr. Bastien to our list of witnesses."

"It's Sunday, and I have to be back to work tomorrow," Marc admonished. "If they release us."

"They should. They have their suspects. At least Lantana Frasier won't come looking for us since Myrtle and Fred are in jail." Connie waved off his concern. "We can't do much here today anyway. Maybe we should head home."

"Reilly was arrested by the feds, tried, and acquitted at the Ashland Federal Courthouse. Perhaps we can find some information in our library there," Polly ventured.

"But we'll need to come back," Connie leaned in.

"I'm off tomorrow and Tuesday," Ethan advised.

Marc had started to take a drink of coffee but lowered it. "Let's not forget that unless Fred and Myrtle are our killers, there is someone desperate enough to kill again out there. I'm not sure I want you back here."

"No one will know what we're doing." Connie waved again.

"I thought you had to go home." Polly wiped a napkin over her mouth.

Connie turned to her, and Polly could have sworn she saw hurt in her sister's eyes. "You sound as if that's what you want me to do."

Polly blinked. Had she sounded that way? Did she want Connie to leave? "No," she answered her thoughts and Connie at the same time. "What better way to bond with my sister than over murder?" She did her best attempt to offer her sister a you're gonna love what I have to say kind of smile that Connie so often gifted to them. Then she turned to Marc. "Honey, we'll be careful. I'll keep in contact with you."

Marc turned a steely gaze to their son. "You'll keep Mom and your aunt safe?"

Ethan widened his eyes. "Sure. No one's gonna hurt Mom or Aunt Connie."

That was her boy.

The front door opened, and two individuals walked in. The tall and hefty woman in front had the same bouffant blond beehive that she sported in the woods. The other individual, a man, tall like the woman but gangly, wore a beige cowboy hat over his dark hair—if the sideburns were any indication of the color. His tie was a bolo. He resembled a country singer and not a Kentucky state policeman, assuming he was an officer.

"Detectives." A waitress provided the answer as she breezed by with a tray of food. "Good to see you back again."

"Good food brings us back every time." The man tipped his hat.

"Gonna tell him to take that hat off, Mom?" Ethan snickered. "As president of the Good Manner's Society, isn't that one of your duties?"

Marc cleared his throat but had trouble hiding his smile behind the napkin he brought up to his face.

Polly leaned forward. "Part of having good manners is not addressing them with strangers who may or may not know better. You, on the other hand . . ."

Ethan laughed and stared upward.

Polly sensed movement behind her and turned. "Good morning, Detective Frasier."

"Morning to you all, too. Thanks for staying over, but with the Conrads in jail, I think we can find you if we need you."

Connie nearly bounced to turn around in her seat. "Do you really think they killed that man?"

The male officer sidled around Detective Frasier, but he remained silent.

"Well, I didn't want to rule out a Bigfoot, but when we found the money box in their possession, what choice did we have?" Detective Frasier placed her hands on her hips, but Polly sensed she was truly asking the question.

"Couldn't it have been planted?" Ethan asked.

"Wouldn't fingerprints tell you if they held it?"

"Right smart one," the man finally spoke. "You should join the force."

"Callahan," Detective Frasier said the name under her breath. Then she smiled at Ethan. "We have them dead to rights, young man. No way they can weasel out of this one. They joined your so-called expedition and waited out Jantzen. When he finally recalled where he'd buried the box, they waited for him to dig it up, and they murdered him for it."

"So, are the feds working this investigation, too?" Connie pushed. "Or are the state police in charge."

"No money, so no feds." Frasier waved her off. "You all have a good day and a nice trip home. I sure am going to enjoy the same." She moved away with her gangly friend following her.

"I'm glad we didn't find the box," Ethan mumbled. "We'd all be in jail."

The detectives turned back.

"No, son," Marc admonished. "We would not. If we'd have found it, we would have turned it over to the police."

The fact that Marc didn't insist that Ethan apologize told Polly her husband somewhat agreed with their son.

The detectives started away.

"So," an old farmer raised his cup of coffee in the

detectives' direction. "Porter and Dolly, where you playing next?"

Callahan laughed and played at strumming an invisible guitar.

Detective Frasier patted her bouffant hair. "Jimmy Jo's in Ashland. Next Saturday."

Connie had taken a sip of coffee. She spit it out.

Right onto Polly.

Polly's steps gained a perk in them as she entered her home in front of Marc and Connie. Evening church services had been a welcome reprieve from the events of the preceding hours of the weekend, and dinner at their favorite restaurant had added to the pleasurable time.

Ethan had joined up with his friends after dinner, so the adults were home alone.

"What say we get up early, have breakfast, and get to the library?" Connie asked.

"Sounds like a plan," Polly agreed. She didn't want to talk about the mystery though. The service had brought some peace to her soul, and she wanted it to remain there.

"Can we talk?" Connie stopped at the foot of the stairs. "After I change. The three of us?"

Maybe working on the mystery was the better plan, but Connie had gone to the woods with them, was staying to help solve the mystery, and Polly owed her sister her ear. "Sure." She looked to her husband.

Marc nodded. "I need to change too. Give me five."

"Make it ten." Polly smiled. "And I'll brew us some tea. Meet up in the kitchen . . ." She checked her watch. ". . . at 8:00 p.m. sharp."

Connie wagged her head as if to let Polly know she was being silly and headed up the stairs.

Marc caught Polly's hand as Connie's door closed. "Listen to her," Marc whispered. "Really listen to her."

Polly held her breath and felt her heart hold back a beat as well. "Is something wrong?"

Marc shook his head. "No, but I know what she's going to talk about is a touchy subject for you."

Anger replaced worry. "You two have been talking about me and what's best for me behind my back."

Marc placed his hands on her shoulders. "No. I let Connie voice what she'd like to talk to you about, and I told her to talk to you. That's the extent of it."

"But you didn't tell me she wanted me at the luncheon," Polly accused. "Perhaps you're not wanting to hear what she has to say either."

He released his hold on her. "I would hope you'd think better of me." He walked up the steps.

Polly followed him into their room. They dressed in silence. Then Polly made her way to their bedroom door to head downstairs to start the tea.

"Polly," Marc said.

She turned without answer.

"I didn't want you broadsided at that luncheon. Connie has a way of pushing your buttons, and I wanted the two of you to sit down and communicate like adults. You couldn't do that if she said what she had to say in the presence of others. I'll support you in any decision you make if only for the reason that you left a successful career to become an equally successful wife and mother of our child."

Polly's eyes filled with tears, and she stepped back to her husband, flinging her arms around his neck. "I love you, Marc Reagan, with all my heart. And being your wife and Ethan's mother is a blessing to me."

"And I love you, Polly Reagan, and I admire everything you do." He kissed her forehead. "Can we have some of your apple pie to go with the tea? I especially admire your apple pie."

"Absolutely." She twirled around and headed downstairs where she happily prepared the pie and brewed the tea.

A knot formed in her throat. She swallowed it down hard. What could Connie possibly have to talk to her about that Marc thought Polly would feel blindsided by it?

Chapter Nine

Back to Reality

Polly sat and cut a fork through her piece of pie. The last one to belly up to the table, she marveled at Marc's quick devourment of his slice.

He leaned back and patted his belly. "I'm one spoiled man, Connie."

Connie nodded but seemed far away in thought.

"What is it you wanted to talk to me about?" Polly prodded. "I suspect it has something to do with why you wanted me at the luncheon."

Connie's features cleared, and she seemed to be in the moment. "Yes, it is."

"I'm all ears." Polly took a large bite of pie, anything to keep her mouth busy while her sister spilled whatever she had to say.

Connie wiggled in her seat and leaned against the table with her arms folded. "I'd like you to think about going beyond being The Foundation's liaison for the children's behavioral center. I'd like you to be legal liaison between the two. I know from communicating with Marc about the endowment that he has his hands full with patients and the everyday run of the place."

"Yes, he does." Polly swallowed her pie and took a sip of tea. "I had already agreed to act as simple liaison. What is it that I would be responsible to do in that capacity?"

"Take care of the legal aspects. Make sure everything is on the up-and-up between the Wright Foundation and the center. Any myriad of details."

"On a volunteer basis?" Polly sent her gaze to Marc.

"We wouldn't want you to get paid or anything like that." Marc winked. "I have some money in the budget to hire in-house counsel and possibly one individual as support staff to oversee not only this endowment but to secure future grants and gifts to the facility. You'd make nowhere near what you made in private practice, but it wouldn't be full-time either."

Polly sent her attention back to her sister. "Why is it so important to you that it be me?"

"I trust you." Connie sighed. "Does it have to be any more complicated than that?"

Marc tapped his knuckle against the table as if to gain Connie's attention. "I think it does, Connie, only because I think there is more to it. Why don't you tell Polly exactly what's on your mind?"

Connie gave Marc a playful glare. "What happened to doctors keeping counsel?"

"Since when am I your doctor?" He chuckled and set his fork on his empty plate.

"Spell it out," Polly encouraged. "I won't know if I agree or not unless you tell me. Make your case."

Connie sat up and took a deep breath. "Okay, Polly. Here goes." She leaned forward. "Ethan's going to school at the end of the summer, and I'm worried that you're going to suffer from that syndrome of over-involved parents."

Polly cut another bite of pie and chewed.

"My thinking is that in acting as a liaison between the center and The Foundation it will fill in some of your time and take the pain of Ethan's absence away from you." She eyed the ceiling for a long moment and took a deep breath. "I don't want you to feel that loss." A tear trickled down her sister's cheek. "I watched Mom go through it when Paul went off to college. She didn't have anything to replace the busy days when she had school kids in the house, and Dad didn't know how to handle it. Oh, they survived, and Mom and I started traveling with

Dad on all The Foundation business. But, frankly, I'm worried that you and Marc might not." She waved her hand in front of her face as if trying to dry the tears. "Her world revolved around us kids, and Mom had a really hard time when I left too." She puffed out her cheeks and let the air out. "I know you're an awesome lawyer. If you use your talents to work for The Foundation and the behavioral center, I could even ask you some legal advice on other issues on occasion."

Polly took a deep breath and let it out. She'd often wondered why her sister had remained in Chicago to attend business school. Part of her wanted to believe she'd stayed close to learn the business while attending school. Now, she suspected Connie had sacrificed to give her mother a bit of comfort . . . and Polly loved her sister all the more for it.

Marc held out his hand. "Five-minute break."

"What?" Polly shook off the sadness. "Are you sending us to our rooms?"

"That's exactly what I'm going to do while I have a second piece of that pie. That will give you a moment to think about what's being asked of you, Polly, and Connie could use a little patience-training. When I'm done eating, I'll let you know."

"He really is a psych geek, isn't he?" Connie stood and pushed her chair under the table.

Polly linked her arm with her sister and led her from the room. Outside the kitchen, she stopped and held her finger to her lips.

Leaning back to see if Marc watched them, she found him absorbed in pulling the pie from the refrigerator.

Connie leaned around her.

Marc sat his plate on the counter beside the pie. He moved the fork to slide off one piece, stopped, and moved it over to encompass two pieces.

Polly smiled at her sister and started up the stairs again. "I always knew he was the midnight double-slice thief, but he insisted that Ethan was the culprit."

"What did Ethan say about it?"

"Covered for his dad, always." She released her sister and walked toward her room. "See you in five."

In her room, Polly stood in front of the mirror and took stock of herself. When Connie had arrived, Polly dressed as she usually did, and despite wanting to horrify her sister, Polly understood there was a bit of mom-frump going on. She'd gotten used to staying at home, dressing up only when she and Marc went out. When Ethan had been younger, there had been interaction with the other mothers, and Polly had stayed close to a few of them, but during most of Ethan's teenage years, her fashion style had been mom frump. No one looked at her when she dropped the kids off or sat in the car or in the bleachers or in a lawn chair by a tennis court. Why did she need to primp?

And she'd gotten used to not going out. She liked being at home with the anticipation of her son and husband's arrival to a clean house, clean clothes, and dinner on the table.

She swallowed. Hard.

Without Ethan's excessive need for uniforms and other clothes, the laundry would be less. The house wouldn't get so dirty, and with years of practice making dinner for three easy, cooking for two would be a cinch.

Other mothers in her circle had taken up tennis or golf to fill their time as the kids needed them less. A few had gone back to careers or taken jobs for something to do. Polly didn't like sports.

Her world centered around her family.

And she had to stop mothering Ethan sometime. He was approaching adulthood. Marc had admonished her several times in the last year that with everything they'd instilled in him, he would be fine, and if he wasn't, there was nothing else they could have done.

Polly took a stuttering breath and caught her own tears.

She would miss her boy when he wasn't here.

She backed from the mirror and plopped down on

her bed, reaching for the book on her nightstand. She turned it over in her hand. Only a day ago, murder mysteries had only been fun reads. Julie B. Cosgrove's *Leaf Me Alone* had been a way to escape reality.

The series, Relatively Seeking, which centered on amateur genealogists turned sleuths, was hitting close to home. Connie had visited with their own relative, Aunt Fanny, and had been instrumental in solving a murder that occurred while there. Was murder following Connie everywhere she went now?

Polly shivered.

"Okay, girls," Marc called.

Polly headed down the stairs.

Connie was already there, standing by the table and not sitting. Marc stood at the counter as if guarding his empty plate.

Polly pulled out her chair and sat. She stared up at her sister. "You have made a very valid argument."

"And?" Connie pressed.

Marc came behind Polly and massaged her shoulders.

She placed her hands over his. "I'd like to take it under advisement."

Connie's shoulders slumped. "So you can let me down easy after I'm gone?"

"No," Polly said. "My consideration is very serious,

and I'll give you my decision before you leave. I'd like to look into some logistics and legalities. I'd also like to let the thought of returning to work outside the home sink in."

"Fair enough?" Marc asked.

Connie nodded. "Fair enough." She reached for her sister's hand. "And thank you for taking me seriously," Connie added.

Polly stood and wrapped her sister in an embrace. "I do take you seriously. Always."

"Well, good."

"I learned that to not take you seriously opens the doors for more shenanigans."

Connie laughed. "And don't you forget it."

A strange ring filled the house.

"What's that?" Marc asked.

"That's not my mobile ring." Still, Polly searched for her phone, digging through her large purse near the back door.

"Not mine either." Marc patted his pockets.

"You two. I'm younger than you are, and even I recognize that as your house phone." Connie hurried about the house looking for the long-silent contraption.

"Hello."

Polly shared a shrug with her husband. "She found it. I forgot where it was."

"I didn't know we were still paying for the thing."

"Mr. Bastien." Connie's high voice and the name she spoke raised the hairs on Polly's neck. "How did you know to call here? No. This is her sister."

Polly and Marc found Connie—and their phone—in the living room. Polly reached for it, but Marc snatched it from Connie's hand. "Excuse me. Who's calling, please?"

Marc's pressed lips were a sign of great agitation. As a toddler, when Ethan saw them and knew he was the cause, he'd utter, "Uh-oh."

Marc's lips parted. "I'm sorry, sir, but how did you get this number?" He listened for a moment and then shook his head. "I believe my wife already told you that we saw nothing else that we didn't share with the police. I appreciate your concern over Myrtle and Fred, and rest assured, if we remember anything, we'll let the authorities know. Good night." He hung up the phone.

"How did he get our number?" Polly placed her hands on her hips.

"He said he looked it up."

"What? In a phone book? Do they still print those things?" Polly asked.

"Really?" Connie widened her eyes and held up her phone. "The world is at your fingertips, guys."

"Persistent, isn't he?" Polly ignored her sister.

Marc nodded. "I don't want to go back on sanctioning this mystery adventure of yours, but I will ask you to be cautious around that man."

Chapter Ten

Peek-A-Boo Bouffant

Polly sat opposite her sister in the Boyd County Public Library where Polly had spent long hours with Ethan during his childhood, both in picking out books and whenever the library hosted special readings for children.

"Look." Connie trailed a red nail down a newspaper article.

Polly read the copy upside down. They'd already learned that Reilly Jantzen had been brought to trial for robbery of the First National Bank of Louisa, Kentucky six months prior to his death. He had been acquitted just as James Bastien had explained.

Connie scanned the copy. "The robber wore a mask, and he did appear to have a gun. The teller—Myrtle

Conrad—did push the alarm at her station, but the police claimed they never received it. The robber got away without incident."

Connie pushed that paper aside and dug through another.

"Isn't this on the computer?" Polly asked.

"Ah, yeah."

"So we can find this information online?" Polly pushed. "Last night, you did say that the world is at our fingertips, did you not?"

Connie looked up and smiled. "Yeah, we could, and I thought about it, but I thought this was more your speed." She winked. "Actually, I planned this before Ethan was asked to work on his day off. I've been watching you. You guys push each other's buttons, and I wanted to push a few of Ethan's by making him go old-school research."

"Nice." Polly slapped hands with her sister. "But instead, you're exasperating me."

"Sorry." Connie smiled. "But I thought you'd buy right into the old-school routine."

Polly stuck out her tongue.

Connie tapped the paper. "There's a familiar character in our little story."

Polly wrinkled her brows and looked down at the picture of several bystanders outside the courthouse.

Lantana Frasier was hard to miss. "She was interviewed?"

"Detective Lantana Frasier says that despite the lack of identification or the confiscation of the monies stolen, she is certain that the right man is on trial," Connie read.

"I thought that lanky Callahan was more her Mr. Right," Polly quipped.

"Odd that she's in the photo, but I guess she could be hanging out around a federal trial just to see the outcome."

Polly puzzled over Connie's statement. "Not sure what you mean?"

"This isn't her collar," Connie advised. "This is a federal crime. She works for the state police."

Polly nodded. "She might be from Louisa, work in Ashland, and had an interest in a case from her hometown. What was that place where she and Callahan said they'd be performing here in Ashland?"

"Jimmy Jo's." Connie pulled out her phone, brought up her search engine, and typed in the locale. "Real place, and look who's performing this Saturday—Lantana Frasier and Andrew Callahan." She held up the phone. "Do you think they're trying to be Dolly and Porter?"

"Could be going for Tammy and George." Polly shrugged.

"I suppose. Loretta and Conway, they are not."

Polly giggled. "I have to say that your knowledge of classic country is impressive."

"Dad," Connie said the one word that explained it all. "He was a closet fan."

Polly suspected that each of her siblings had specific memories of their parents that belonged to them alone. Polly's was his favorite aftershave, Timberwood, that was her responsibility to buy him each year for Christmas. Mom made the gift buying easy for them. Dad always got the same gifts from each until they were old enough to go shopping on their own, but Dad had pulled her aside one Thanksgiving soon after she'd married. "I didn't get my Timberwood last year, Polly-girl. I missed it."

She'd never forgotten to place it under the tree again. Oh, she'd added surprise gifts, but Dad could always expect to get his Timberwood from her every December.

The year of his death, she had stood in the department store in front of the Timberwood display. Her fingers had trembled as she picked up the bottle and lifted it to her nose. She'd breathed in the wood scent, and for a moment, she could imagine Dad right beside her. She'd bought the bottle, carried it home, and she'd hidden it away in a drawer where she still took it out from time to time.

"I miss him, too." Connie broke into her thoughts.

"How did you know what I was thinking?"

"The tears in the corner of your eyes. They visit me when I think of Mom and Dad."

Polly blinked, and the tears splashed down on her shirt. She wiped the moisture away. Time to change the subject. "That must have been some surprise for Frasier to be called to a state park to investigate a murder and find out that the victim's a suspect from a past robbery in which she showed notable interest." Polly bit her lower lip. "Is it too much of a coincidence?"

"Depends on several factors. She and Callahan seem to be known in that little town. Maybe they work out of there from time to time. I'm sure bank robberies are rare there. Or maybe she's got a burr up her beehive bouffant thinking Jantzen got away with the crime."

"Okay. I'm reading too much into it."

Connie perused the newspapers for a few moments before folding them up and tapping her red nail on the table. "Who are our suspects?"

"We have three: Myrtle, Fred, and . . ."

"Don't say it," Connie warned.

"Well, Frasier didn't come out and say it exactly, but I think he's on her list as well."

"A Bigfoot did not kill that man."

"He wasn't shot. How did he die?"

"He was hit in the head with something."

"The chest, maybe? How heavy would it be with so much money stuffed inside?"

"Too heavy to lift and bash him in the head with it, even if he was on the ground when it was done."

"Unless he'd been knocked down and the box was dropped onto his head."

Connie narrowed her eyes. "Could be, but if they'd dropped it, would it have made a gash like the one on Jantzen's forehead?"

Polly shrugged. "They didn't find anything else. I overheard that there was nothing to indicate that the shovel found at the scene was any more than Reilly's tool for digging. He wasn't hit with it.

"He had a rifle with him out there. Remember? It was near the body."

"The murderer must have hit him with whatever before Reilly knew what had happened."

"Fred is a big man. He could have lifted the box and swung. Say Jantzen had pulled up the box. Fred came upon him and picked it up. Reilly would trust him, and Fred surprised him by using the box as a murder weapon." Polly mimed the incident with her hand being the box. She hit her head and fell back against the chair.

A librarian stopped on her way past them and waved her finger, tsking as she ambled on.

"You're a loon." Connie rolled her eyes but then pointed at her sister. "And that's a good theory."

"What? That I'm a loon?"

"That you're a loon is not a theory. It's conclusive."

Polly smirked and chose to ignore the comment. "Let's take Fred and Myrtle out of the picture. Is there anyone else?"

"Bastien is a little too nervous for my comfort."

Connie pointed. "I was hoping you had the same feeling. He does appear to be very skittish."

"Do you think it's safe to even talk to him?" Polly pressed.

Connie didn't speak. She gathered up the newspapers, left for a few moments, and returned with copies of the articles. "Just in case we want to look at them again. As for speaking with Mr. Bastien, I think we need to avoid talking about our theories. We need to question him while being careful not to give him any new information."

Polly followed Connie through the library. Outside, she shielded her eyes, using her hand as a visor.

A dark sedan caught her attention, and she stared in that direction. The glare, though, kept her from seeing inside.

Connie zigzagged a little and stepped beside Polly. "With Fred and Myrtle in jail, why do you suppose we're being followed by the good lady detective?"

Polly fought to keep from looking in the direction of the car. "You can see her?"

"Well, not her exactly, just the top of her up-do."

She could think of no reason whatsoever that Detective Frasier would have to follow them to the library, of all places. At the car, Polly pushed the fob, unlocked the doors, and sat inside. She busied herself putting on her seatbelt. "Do you think she knows what we were doing here?"

"Not sure." Connie brought her seatbelt around her. "I get the feeling that she's not buying your story about why you've been on the monthly expeditions with those three, and she's trying to find a connection."

"What do we do now?"

"We go by the center and see if Marc's free for lunch. Then we drive by the grocery store where Ethan works in the hope that you and I can embarrass him a little in front of his co-workers, and we remind him that unless he wants to miss the trip to Louisa tomorrow, he better not agree to work. Who gave him such a work ethic anyway?"

Polly laughed. "I think he has some really good genes." Polly started the car. "And, by the way, Old Hairy is still a suspect in my book. Though I think the people in that area think she's Old Harriet."

Connie scrunched her nose. "They think they can tell?"

Polly backed out of her spot and left the parking lot. "If Myrtle's comments are any indication. She called it a her."

Connie settled in her seat. "I believe your friend is a bit touched if you ask me."

Polly sat on the bed with her laptop opened as she researched exactly what might be expected of her as a legal liaison for the Jimmy Reagan Children's Behavioral Center.

Yes, Marc would be her boss—no problem there, but she had learned early on in her career to set boundaries for herself and others. When she had "retired" to raise Ethan, she'd been far from burned out. She'd been a go-getter, and she strived to do the best she could for the firm.

Marc would expect nothing less.

She typed out her job expectations and wishes, her hours, and even her requested starting salary, keeping it low because, after all, the center was a labor of love for her husband who had mourned the loss of his beloved only nephew due to a drug overdose. Soon after Jimmy's death, his father, James, had died in a car accident. The center had been a way of coping with the grief for Marc.

The door opened, and Marc stepped inside. He rubbed his belly. "When did you find time to make another pie?"

"Did the two-slice thief invade the refrigerator again?" She tilted her head and smiled.

"Yeah, he did. I'll have to talk to him about that. It's a compulsion, you know."

"Spoken like a true psychiatrist. What will you prescribe for him?"

"Just say no." He winked. "But his willpower is lacking, darn near non-existent."

She giggled as he sat on the bed and leaned over.

"Whatcha doing, Polly-my-love?" he asked.

She laid against him. "I promised Connie I'd make a decision. I've done a little research into median pay, the job descriptions for most of the titles that encompass the work I'd be doing, and I've been looking at the time I think it would take me per week."

Marc kissed the top of her head. "Don't let your sister talk you into something you aren't ready to do. And, as she said, you are an excellent lawyer. Time doesn't change that. Even if you entered the workforce on a lower level, I imagine that you could be at the top of your field again in no time. You might even consider changing course, working for the state in some capacity."

Polly turned to catch his eye. "You're not trying to find a gentle way to tell me that you don't want me working for the center, are you?"

Marc blinked. "No. No. Why would you say that? I'd be a fool not to want someone with your caliber of expertise in my corner."

"It seems like you're trying to talk me out of it?"

A slow smile started in one corner of his lips and moved across to the other side.

Polly narrowed her eyes. "What's so amusing, Marc Reagan?"

He shook his head. "First of all, I'm giving you the alternatives because I want you to be fully aware that there are other paths for you. I often find that people who are unhappy—especially those that I treat—feel stuck. You'd never be stuck in the job at the center. You could always leave, but I'd find it hard to replace you. And, you know, you don't have to do any of this. If your happiness is found in taking care of our home and me for the rest of your life, I'm satisfied."

"But you'd be better helped by your helpmate if she worked alongside you . . ." Polly threw her arms around his neck and kissed his cheek. "Marc Reagan, I love you so much."

"So, you've made your decision it seems." He raised

his brows and then wiggled them. "You choose me."

"I always choose you. But whether I work at home or for the center, no, I haven't made my decision. You'll be the first to know, though."

"Fair enough." He scooted from the bed.

At the bathroom door he paused and turned. "Be careful in Louisa, okay? I have a bad feeling about whatever's going on there."

Polly stood and moved to him. "So do I, but I have a larger feeling deep inside me that if I don't do anything, there's an elderly man and woman who may never see the outside of a prison. I'd like to understand why and how Fred and Myrtle were helping Reilly."

"If they were at all," Marc said. "Bastien could be pushing suspicion in their direction. He's antsy about something."

Polly had been leery of James Bastien.

Marc touched her face with his hand. "Please be careful tomorrow because wherever you end up, you are an absolute necessity to me."

Polly leaned into his touch. "I was beginning to worry about that."

"Never, Polly-my-love." He kissed her long and hard.

"Gross, oh gross!" The squeal rang out from two voices. Connie and Ethan made faces at them from the doorway.

"What are you doing, spying on us?" Polly charged the opened door. "Ever heard of knocking, you two?"

Ethan covered his eyes with his hands. "We were passing by and thought we'd ask you if we could get an early start. And the door was open."

"Down Home Grill seems to have a wealth of information," Connie added.

"And Dee's Drive-Inn." Ethan was definitely a growing boy. His entire existence surrounded the ability to consume food.

"This is not a tour of your favorite Louisa, Kentucky, eateries, Ethan Reagan. We have serious work to do." Polly placed her hand on the door. "And good night." She closed it in her son's and sister's faces before turning into the arms of her husband. "Where were we?"

Marc pointed to the bathroom. "I was going to brush my teeth. What were you doing?" He teased and drew her close. "But I can do that anytime."

The Visitor Meets Old Hairy

Chapter Eleven

The Low Down at the Down Home

Polly glanced in her rearview mirror as they pulled into the parking lot of the Down Home Grill. Ethan was asleep, having awakened only long enough to dress and climb into the backseat of the car. "We're here," she announced.

Her son didn't budge.

Connie swiveled in her seat. "Maybe we should leave him in here, have breakfast, and let him know what he's missed when we return to the car."

"Yeah, more trouble than that's worth. I can always tell when his sugar levels dip. He becomes a two-year-old again." Polly parked the car, undid her seatbelt, and turned to rouse her boy.

He moved only to swing his arm against his eyes.

"Give me a minute."

"Come on, Ethan. We're here. The pancakes and bacon have to be calling your name." Polly tugged her purse from behind her seat and opened her car door. She slid out of her seat, and just as she'd silently predicted, Ethan's feet hit the parking lot before her own did.

He was also the first to the door, holding it open for Polly and Connie.

They entered with a "Welcome" called from somewhere inside the restaurant.

A waitress met them with menus in hand. "Your handsome man not with you today?"

Polly turned to look to see if she spoke to someone else.

"You." The woman marched them through the restaurant to a seat by the window. "Ain't you the ones that were part of Reilly's expedition for Bigfoot that turned bad?"

Patrons turned their heads and followed them with seemingly curious gazes.

Ethan ducked his head a little lower.

"Yeah, we were," Connie announced a bit too loudly.

"Geesh, Aunt Connie," Ethan muttered.

"Turned out badly for Reilly . . ." Connie started.

"Turned out worse for Myrtle and Fred." A man

wearing an International Harvester tractor ballcap bobbed his head. "No way I'll ever believe they killed somebody—and for money. That crazy Lantana Frasier should know that."

Connie sat at the far seat facing the old man. Polly sat beside her, and Ethan kept his back to the crowd, his head hung low.

"Is she from here?" Connie asked in a matter-of-fact way.

"Born and raised in Fort Gay, across the rivers, but she moved on to Ashland right after she got on with the state police. Comes here a lot, though."

"On patrol or investigation?" Connie continued the conversation.

The amount of spit that came with the pffths from the room could have filled up a jar, but no one explained.

A teenage waitress sauntered to the table, her attention never leaving Ethan. "Coffee, tea or . . .?"

Ethan managed to lift his gaze, but Polly had raised him better than to give his order before the women.

"Coffee," Polly and Connie said at once.

"Sweet tea for me," Ethan told her.

She smiled the warmest smile Polly had ever seen—all of it directed at Ethan who lowered his head again.

The girl's smile vanished as she departed, and Polly kicked him under the table. At the same time, Connie elbowed him.

"Ouch!" Ethan pulled back. "Why'd you two do that?"

"Give the girl a smile, will ya?" Connie glared.

"Did you see him?" The man in the International Harvester hat raised his coffee mug in their direction.

"See who?" Polly asked.

"Old Hairy—Bigfoot."

Polly tossed a seriously stern look in her sister's direction.

"Yeah, they did!" Ethan rang out. "Tell them, Mom."

Now, Polly lowered her gaze to the table.

Quiet filled the restaurant.

The young girl returned with the drinks and waited—for what? Their orders or the telling of the story?

Ethan smiled at her, and the girl's brilliant smile returned. "What can I get you?"

They placed their orders. The waitress read it back to them and then stepped away.

"I see 'im on occasion."

Polly had expected International Harvester Man to be the one to say so, but it was a thin woman whose braided hair was long enough for her to sit on it.

"He's a big 'un, and I mean big. A hairy thing."

"Yes, ma'am." A teenage boy sat up straight. "He's out there around the dam. Me and my friends were camping out there. We were walking back from the lake with a bunch of fish we'd caught and were gonna fry up. My friend seen him first. He was behind a tree, kinda blended in, but he was bigger 'round. He didn't move unlessen we moved. And we stopped. Tommy wanted to run, but Melvin, he said to hold up. We started squabbling when Melvin took our fish, line and all, and tossed them in the creature's direction. We were mighty mad at him, but he said we weren't staying there anyway, not with that thing hanging out."

"Did he step out and get the fish?" Ethan had hung on every word the boy said.

"Not that we saw. We ran."

Connie stood and looked around. "Anyone else see this thing?"

Others shook their head; some looked down at their plates, as if embarrassed to admit they'd seen anything.

International Harvester Man took off his cap and rubbed his hand through his bristled blond hair. "Can't say I have, but I've heard from those who do claim to have seen him."

"Ma'am," Connie ventured close to the woman who shared her sighting, "do you remember how long ago it was since you spotted the thing?"

"Bigfoot, you mean," the lady corrected. "Yes. I started seeing him about two months ago. The last time was about three weeks back."

"And you, sir?" Connie pointed to the teenage boy.

"About three weeks ago, too. But others have been saying they've seen him. I think the reports go back a few months now."

The waitress returned with their order.

"Thank you. We came looking for information to help Fred and Myrtle, and I think you folks have given us what we need."

"So," International Harvester Man put his hat back on his head and rubbed his chin. "You think Bigfoot went and killed the likes of Reilly Jantzen?"

Connie smiled her you're going to love what I have to say smile. "No, sir. I do not."

Polly breathed a sigh of relief, though she hadn't expected anything different from her sister.

"But we do believe he's involved in some way."

Polly jolted.

Uncomfortable laughter filtered through the restaurant.

"We do?" Polly asked.

"Yes." Connie's smile nearly wrapped around her ears.

"We really do?" Ethan asked.

"We really, really do." Connie bowed her head.

Polly said grace.

"Lord, we really, really do," Connie said. "Now, please help me prove it."

The *Visitor* Meets Old Hairy

Chapter Twelve

He Walks These Woods

Back in the car in the diner's parking lot, Polly kept her hand on the ignition without turning the key. "What was that in there? Are you playing with those poor people?"

Ethan closed his door. "Mom, you said you all saw a Bigfoot. Why couldn't they?"

Polly situated herself so she could see both her sister and her son. "We saw something." She sighed. "We saw and heard something large and hairy, but even though, on occasion, I'm willing to say that it was a Bigfoot, something inside of me knows there's another explanation. That boy and that woman believe they saw the real thing, and Connie fed into that unwavering belief when I know she doesn't think Bigfoot exists." She nudged her sister. "You don't believe Old Hairy killed or helped to kill Reilly."

"No, but someone who wants people to believe a Bigfoot is out there did." Connie high-fived Ethan. "And we're going to find out just who that is so that we can provide some peace to these folks."

Polly breathed a sigh of relief and sent a prayer of thanks to the Lord. "So where to next?"

Connie didn't answer for a moment. She swiveled in her seat and looked around her. Seemingly satisfied, she faced forward. "Let's go to the lake and take a walk."

"Why start there?" Ethan asked as Polly started the car.

"Because, Nephew, the longer we're in town, the more chance we have of being seen, and I want to look into visiting Myrtle in jail. I have a better chance of that if the detectives don't think I'm nosing into their business. Ethan, get on your phone and see what we need to do in order to see her."

Ethan tapped away on his phone.

"Polly, let's drive out there, take a walk, and see if we can locate the murder site again. I have a feeling there are clues that have been missed."

Polly did as her sister asked and drove to Yatesville Lake. She parked in the main parking lot. They could walk rather than drive into the campsite where their presence might be too obvious.

Outside the car, Polly took in the area while she waited for her sister and her son to exit. "Ethan knows his way around the lake and can walk us into the camping area. We'll let him lead."

"Myrtle and Fred are in the Big Sandy Regional Detention Center in Paintsville," Ethan announced. "But here's the thing. We don't have to visit them in person. We can set up a video phone call."

Polly smirked. "Technology making it easy to stay in touch with your favorite criminal."

Connie wagged her finger. "There are innocent people in jail—like Fred and Ethel."

"Myrtle," Polly corrected. "And you are right."

"Ethan, set up that call, will you?" Connie opened her car door.

"That will keep any nosy people from knowing that we've visited with them." Polly was finding herself breathing sighs of relief all over the place.

"Not exactly." Connie met her at the front of the car. "They keep a log. If Detective Frasier wanted to see who called, she could ask for the records."

"Do you really think she cares?" Ethan joined them.

"Not sure yet, but unlike Old Hairy, I want to keep our footprint trail as small and invisible as possible." Connie fell into step behind her nephew.

"I've set it up for tomorrow morning."

"Good job." Connie patted his back. "And I think if Detective Frasier is curious, it's only about visitors of suspects she may think are accomplices."

"We've only seen her once. We may be over-inflating her attention to us," Polly said.

Connie didn't answer but took the lead, leaving Polly and Ethan to follow her.

"Do you know where you're going?" Polly baited.

Connie stopped with her left hand pointing out. "Lake this way. Camp that way?"

Ethan laughed and pointed in the other direction. "Camp's that way, Aunt Connie."

"Know it all." Connie laughed and let Ethan have the lead while she followed with Polly.

"You're enjoying yourself, admit it," Polly teased.

"I'll admit it. I love a good mystery."

They stayed silent as they walked the path. It was a much longer hike than she'd thought. They finally came upon the camping area. She put her hands over the back of her head and drew in a deep breath and pushed it out.

Ethan paused. "You okay, Mom."

"Peachy," she said between breaths and pointed toward the woods. "Keep going."

Ethan continued leading the way through the path between the trees until they came upon the familiar.

Nothing would have denoted the site except for a piece of yellow tape left behind on a limb where Reilly had died. "What are we trying to find?" Polly treaded carefully around the scene.

Connie waved her hand up and down as if indicating the ground. "Isn't this the path we were on when we saw whoever we saw?"

"There abouts. Up a little, and we were just off the path. Remember? You were making enough noise," Polly bantered.

"We had this discussion. The wind was blowing. Nothing could have heard our snapping twigs. And I did a little research last night. Bigfoot doesn't normally take a carved-out path, does he?"

"He follows access points." Ethan lifted his chin with a hint of superior knowledge. "Many sightings have occurred in paths cut for large power lines. Also, he's known to walk ridges. Some Native Americans refer to him as Ridge Walker."

"But would he walk where humans walk? Isn't the natural inclination to shy away?"

Ethan scratched his head. "You're not making sense with your questions, Aunt Connie. If you don't believe he's real, why are you asking what he would do?"

Good question, and one Polly wanted to know. "My kid's pretty smart, don't you think? Care to enlighten us?" She raised her brows at her sister.

"I'm pointing out to you that we didn't see Bigfoot. What we saw was a human being dressed as a Bigfoot."

"A very convincing costume if you ask me." Polly leaned against a tree.

"Has to be. Other people have reported seeing this person, and those individuals are convinced it's a creature." Connie continued to search the area.

"Why couldn't it be a real Bigfoot?" Ethan asked.

Connie shook her head and stared wide-eyed. "Really, Ethan? You believe that a seven-to-eight-foot hairy creature walks these woods?"

Ethan blushed under his aunt's steel gaze, but he nodded. "Before the murder, I didn't. But now, I believe."

Polly wanted to sidle up beside her son and confess her belief, too. Instead, she remained silent.

"He does walk these woods. And if I was you, I'd think twice before coming out here unarmed."

Polly jolted and tucked her nearly grown son behind her.

She had not heard Lantana Frasier draw close to them, and Polly almost wanted to apologize to her sister about the noise comment. Clearly, twigs could snap, and no one would notice. There would be no way that someone as large as Lantana Frasier could walk undetected through the woods, and she clearly had not taken a path. Or had she been here unseen this entire time?

"Just why are you out here?" The detective eyed them.

"Curiosity." Connie straightened. "What about you, Detective?"

Lantana hefted her body, making her cleavage bounce.

Connie held the detective's stare. "We're just looking around. I'm visiting my sister, and, well, I wanted to see the area."

"I wanted to look at the structure." Ethan pointed in the direction of the habitat the police had discovered the night of the murder. "It proves our expedition was a success."

Connie stepped closer to the detective. "What did you mean when you said he walks these woods?"

The detective smiled and seemed to relax. "I've seen him out here. He's very impressive and scary."

"Agreed," Polly said. "And that howl?"

Frasier startled. "You didn't hear him howl." She swallowed. "Did you?"

"Yes, we did." Polly pointed this time. "He was up there a ways and seemed to be following a skunk. He stopped in front of us and let out a chilling howl."

The detective looked around her. "I don't think I'd like to hear that."

Connie turned to Ethan. "The two of us are on opposing sides of the Bigfoot theory. I don't believe in them. He does. I suspect my sister does, too, but she's afraid to outright admit it."

"But you saw him, too, didn't you say?"

"I saw something, Detective." Connie paused and seemed to size up Frasier. "I'm not sure who it was, but I'm determined to find out."

"Well, I'll leave you to your exploring." The detective started away again.

"Detective Frasier," Polly called.

Frasier turned. "Yes, ma'am."

"We had nothing to do with Reilly Jantzen's murder. I'd never met any of the other expedition members outside of my family before the expeditions began. I certainly didn't know he had been tried for robbery or that he had a criminal history."

"Tried and acquitted," Connie added. "Which means he may not have been involved."

Ethan moved to the area of the empty hole. He stooped down but didn't touch anything.

Frasier took a step back toward them. Her eyes were slits. "He was involved. He dug up the box later found in the possession of the Conrads. They were in this together.

She was an insider in the bank. He took and hid it, and the fool forgot where. They were out here looking, and because it was too suspicious, they had to draw in some dolts as cover and pretend they were out here looking for Old Hairy. Reilly found the box, and the old couple killed him so they wouldn't have to share the money."

"But the box was empty." Connie placed her hands on her hips while asking the rhetorical question. "The funds were unrecovered both when Reilly was arrested, by the FBI, and when he was murdered, which is your investigation. Odd thing, huh?"

"Is that why you're out here?" The detective fixed a stare on all three of them. "You thinking you want to take a bit of cash home with you?"

Connie straightened. "We could ask the same of you."

"And of the four of us, which one has the authority to be out here looking for stolen cash?" Frasier challenged.

"Neither one of us." Connie straightened.

Frasier remained silent.

"That's right, Detective. You might be out here to follow up on the murder investigation, but the stolen money—that belongs to the FBI."

Frasier hesitated. Then she placed her hands on her hefty waist. "You sure you want to be out here? Bad things can happen to people alone in the woods."

"Is that a threat?" Ethan stood and drew closer.

Polly touched his arm, drawing him back.

Frasier didn't seem to notice. "You've seen him once. You want to see him again?"

Ethan turned his back and started to walk away. "I'd love to see him. I'm going to look at his structure."

"You may get what you asked for, son. I'd be careful." Frasier yelled and pointed at Ethan, turned, and made her way down the path.

Polly and Connie caught up with Ethan at the makeshift lair.

Ethan stared at the tangle of huge trees.

"What's on your mind?" Polly asked.

He touched an impossible bend in the tree limb. "I don't know what to believe about Bigfoot, but I do know that a human being could not do this."

"At least without an explanation." Connie examined the structure. "But once we learn the how of it, the impossible becomes the possible."

Ethan's smile didn't reach his eyes. "What if the impossible was the possible?"

Polly drew near. "What do you mean?"

"What if the impossibility of a Bigfoot was the possible?"

Polly stretched her imagination, but not far. After

all, she'd seen the creature.

"Mom?" Ethan pulled her from her thoughts.

"Yes."

"Have you ever heard of cryptozoology?"

"Something about the science of creatures not really known to exist." Polly smiled. "But I'm not sure how you science something you can't find."

"I'd like to learn how. Do you think Dad would be really upset if I didn't go to med school to become a psychiatrist?"

"You're not interested in that any longer?" The question came from Connie.

"Yeah, I am." Ethan pulled at a stubborn leaf on a limb. "But I'm more interested in majoring in cryptozoology."

Polly faltered.

Marc had taken a big step in allowing his family to investigate a murder, but she wasn't so sure how he'd respond when he learned that his only son wanted a career researching the seemingly impossible.

The *Visitor* Meets Old Hairy

Chapter Thirteen

Hypothetically Speaking

With Ethan saving a seat at Dee's Drive-Inn and the added mission of listening to or engaging others about the death of Reilly Jantzen, Polly held open the door for her sister to enter the First National Bank of Louisa, Kentucky.

She stepped toward the information desk intending to ask if Mr. Bastien was available, but Bastien, himself, beat her to the kiosk. His gaze shifted from her to Connie and back again. "Are you here to see me?"

"Yes, if you have a moment or two. We can't be long. Someone's waiting for us." She didn't want to give the man too much information.

"I have all the time you need. Have you thought of any new information?" He led them across the lobby toward a corner office.

Polly slid a glance to her sister who stepped beside her as they followed the bank manager.

Mr. Bastien turned as if awaiting an answer.

She faltered a bit and glanced at Connie. "While we haven't recalled anything, we were hoping that you could provide us with a little information about the robbery."

Bastien showed them into his office and motioned for them to take a seat while he lifted his more-than-ample body around the desk. "I don't know why you need to know anything about that."

Connie slid forward in her seat and folded her hands on top of the table. "Mr. Bastien, I don't for one minute believe that Ethel killed Mr. Jantzen."

Mr. Bastien shook his head. "Ethel? You suspect Myrtle because this Ethel isn't someone you could see killing Jantzen?"

Polly would have laughed out loud, but she wanted to show a little decorum. "My sister is thinking of characters in an old sitcom and pairing the names. She meant that we don't suspect Myrtle or Fred. Therefore, we're thinking that if we had some more details about the robbery, we might be able to check on some leads."

Bastien swiveled his chair. "Wouldn't those leads best be located by the authorities?" he challenged.

"You mean the authorities that arrested Fred and

Eth—I mean Fred and Myrtle? Those authorities?" Connie challenged. "I trust them even less than I trust you."

Whoa! Connie had left polite conversation and had gone for the jugular. She thought her sister was only that direct when dealing with people who tried to manipulate one of their charities for their own benefit.

"You don't trust me?" Mr. Bastien's face fell. "I'm a solid, outstanding citizen. Fred and I are deacons at our church. Myrtle has been a mentor to my wife." He patted this stomach. "I didn't come by this girth without Myrtle teaching my Tonya how to cook."

Connie seemed to relax. "You can understand that your tracking us down and seeking out information makes you a little suspicious, can't you?"

Bastien didn't speak for a moment. Then he smiled. "I guess I did come on a little too strong, but Tonya is beside herself thinking of Myrtle in a jail cell, and Fred is too kind of a man to be behind bars."

"Was Myrtle pretending to help Reilly locate the money so she could prove that Reilly was the robber? Did she suspect that he'd hidden the money in the woods?" Polly asked.

Bastien picked up a pen on his desk and examined it. He shifted in his seat. "Ladies, Reilly confessed to Myrtle that he took the money. Myrtle was out there to find it, yes. Please don't ask me to betray my friends any more than I have just now."

"Seems to me that you want us to find bogus information to clear your friends who're just as guilty as Reilly." This time, Polly wasn't pulling any punches. Maybe her sister was rubbing off on her.

Connie unfolded her hands and patted the desk, her red nails clicking on the wood with each pat. "All we're asking for is the truth in order to understand what form of help Myrtle was giving to Reilly that wouldn't make her an accomplice in the bank robbery."

"I'm sorry, ladies. I can't betray a confidence such as the one that Myrtle and Fred entrusted me."

The man's language had become a little flowery. Bastien pulled on his tie.

Connie pressed a red fingernail to her lip.

A thought crossed Polly's mind. The biggest aha she'd had in some time. "Maybe that's not what was happening at all."

Connie scooted in her chair to look at Polly. "Go on."

Polly thought for a moment. They'd discussed not giving up theories to Mr. Bastien, but maybe if she shared with him, he'd open up to them.

"What if, as you say, the Bigfoot expedition was a cover for Reilly. This was our third month out there. He started the expeditions soon after his acquittal. Perhaps he wanted the ruse to play out so that when the time was right, he could dig up the goods. He probably knew where he'd buried it, but to go after it first off and to stop the expedition would have raised suspicion."

Connie leaned back in her seat and stared Bastien in his eyes. "And Myrtle and Fred patiently waited for him to find it. They hid out in the woods, and they watched. Maybe that's why they were helping Reilly, and you knew about that. You want us to believe that Myrtle and Fred are accomplices to the robbery so that we'll believe they also murdered Jantzen. That way, you get away clean as an ogler's whistle."

Polly stood and paced. "The authorities would have found other holes from earlier expeditions and attempts to locate it if Reilly hadn't known where he'd buried it. So that theory holds water."

Connie turned her attention to Polly. "They didn't find the money in the box. Fred and Myrtle had to hide the cash somewhere in order to get it out of the woods." She beaded in once again on Bastien. "Or they had help getting it out of there. Maybe all three of these people are guilty, and only two of them aren't trying to frame the other one."

Bastien raised his hands. "Ladies, you're way off base here. Neither of us robbed this bank or framed anyone, and your wild ideas aren't going to do a world of good."

"Then why don't you tell us the truth?" Polly edged.

"Perhaps the ones you need to speak with are the ones who can tell you firsthand what was going on. I've said it already, and I'll say it again. I was given a confidence. I'm not one who gives those up easily. If Fred or Myrtle had authorized me to tell you what was going on, I would."

"Even if their lives depended upon it?" Connie pressed. "You wouldn't tell the authorities either?"

"I wouldn't tell them a thing. No." He stood.

"Thank you, Mr. Bastien." Connie stood abruptly.

"Please assure me that you won't go to the police with your assumptions. I'll admit they are good ones, but they are not valid. If you're going to dig into this, please do Fred, Myrtle, and me the courtesy of finding the truth."

Connie led Polly to the door but stopped. "Do you have a plausible theory?"

Mr. Bastien drew near. "Of course. I've had a working theory on this since right after the trial."

Connie blocked Polly's exit. "What's that theory?"

"That Bigfoot herself was involved from the start, and she did Reilly Jantzen in."

Polly feathered an uneasy chuckle. "You think that

the Bigfoot in the woods is a woman?"

"I know for a fact she is." He led them to the front door. "But I need for you to come to that conclusion on your own. Floating that theory can be pretty dangerous for a bank manager. I'm sure you can see that."

Polly could see that. After all, for a moment during Frasier's interrogation, she'd thought that she'd endangered Marc's career at the center.

"Thank you, Mr. Bastien. We'll let you know if we find anything else that might help." Connie pushed Polly out the door.

"Please do." He waved them off.

As they left the bank, Connie snapped her fingers and pointed to the sky. "We need to get back out there to the murder scene."

The Visitor Meets Old Hairy

Chapter Fourteen

Doubling Back

Polly never liked dealing with her son when his sugar levels were low. She peered at him in her rearview mirror as he sat in the backseat.

"I don't see why we couldn't have at least ordered. I sat there smelling the food for a half hour." Ethan was hunched down, arms crossed, and a scowl on his face. "We couldn't have just gotten something to go?"

Polly stared at Connie, and when her sister felt her gaze and glanced at her, Polly raised her eyebrows. "Good question."

"I suppose we could have. Do you want to go back, or should we go out to the woods, see if I can find what I'm looking to find, and then go back to Dee's?"

"Go back to Dee's now," Polly said. To her surprise,

Ethan demanded the same thing at the same time.

Polly pulled to the side of the road and turned the car around. As she started to merge into the lane heading back toward Louisa, Polly spotted a dark sedan off the road behind some trees. It had been hidden as they drove toward the lake, but turning around, she could see it easily.

She touched Connie's arm and pointed toward the vehicle. "We need to get back to town. Do you think we've been followed or is it just a coincidence that the car is parked there?"

"Ethan," Connie said, "your mom and I are going to stare ahead as if we don't see the vehicle. From your seat behind me, you may not be seen. Look at the car, will you, and tell us if anyone's inside."

"Sure," Ethan scrunched further against the side of the car.

Polly turned onto the road and drove past.

"I didn't see anyone inside." Ethan seemed to sigh in relief. "Maybe we shouldn't be out here, though. I'm not feeling too good about this."

Connie waved her hand as though his concerns were just gnats. "We'll get something to eat and decide what to do from there. We have the call with Myrtle tomorrow. Maybe she can help us in some way."

"Dad might have some ideas," Ethan offered.

"Good idea," Polly concurred. "Let's get some grub and head home."

Connie didn't answer, but she didn't argue either.

Polly steered the car back to town and pulled into Dee's Drive-Inn. They walked into the restaurant again and took a table.

"You're back." A man behind the counter pointed and grinned at Ethan. "You gonna eat this time or just take up space again?"

"I'm gonna eat, and twice as much as I would have if these two hadn't pulled me out of here."

Polly chose a table and sat down. Connie and Ethan followed. They placed their orders, and the food was up quickly.

Ethan bit into his Dee's hamburger with a relish and swiped his arm across his mouth. Then he used the napkin to wipe the ketchup from his arm.

Polly breathed in deeply and released the air slowly. "I believe I've raised you better than that."

"Did you?" Ethan laughed. "Or did I just now do that?"

Connie laughed aloud. "You two are a hoot." She smacked at Ethan's arm and messed his hair. "Can't say that I don't enjoy the camaraderie you share."

The man behind the counter came around to their table. "Excuse me, but when this young man was in here earlier, one of my regulars said that you might have been the folks out at the lake when Reilly Jantzen was killed. Is that true?"

Not again.

Connie's face lit up. "Yes, we were there."

The man nodded to the chair, and Polly nodded back. He pulled out the seat and sat. "Good time to take a break. We have a lull this time of day."

"Do you know Myrtle and Fred?" Connie asked.

"Who doesn't know those two loveable goofballs? They're a town treasure. Myrtle used to have a nice word for everyone who entered the bank, and Fred, he was known as the best foreman at the coal plant. He knew everyone in need, and he worked to supply the need. Many a family have had Christmas left at their door, and everyone knew, without him saying, who left it there."

"Not a murderer then?" Connie took a sip of her soft drink.

"Not on your life, ma'am. Word around here is that Bigfoot was at the scene. Do you happen to know about that?"

"We have no idea if Bigfoot was at the scene of the murder. He was probably hiding out if he was there." Polly smiled.

The man chuckled. "You ain't from these parts, are you?"

"Ashland," Polly answered. "We were part of Reilly Jantzen's Bigfoot expedition. It was a way to relax once a month and spend time with my son before he goes to college in September."

"The folks in town have a pretty good idea what's going on, but if we told you, your life wouldn't be worth that plug nickel everyone talks about but no one has ever seen. You need to be careful."

"Do you know Detective Lantana Frasier?" Polly took another sip and stared over the lid of her cup.

"Sure do." He stood and pushed his chair under the table. "She's larger than life, don't you think?" He moved back behind the counter and then out of sight.

Ethan blinked and stared at his aunt. "We gotta get back to the lake."

"What? Why?" Polly sputtered. "I thought we'd decided to go home, get your dad's opinion, speak to Myrtle tomorrow, and then go from there."

"The kid's right. We're wasting daylight." Connie paid for their meals, and they headed back outside.

"I'm not sure about this," Polly countered. "I like our first plan best."

"That wasn't a plan." Ethan waited by the car. "We were mulling things over. Mom, we gotta get out there."

"For what?"

"Don't you know?" Connie laughed.

"No, I do not know, Connie. Why don't you enlighten me?"

"I'd rather Old Hairy do that. Now, let's go."

Chapter Fifteen

We Are Not Alone

Lookout. That was Polly's job, but she wanted to be a part of the search as well—though she wasn't sure exactly what Connie and Ethan were looking for, and neither had mentioned it while in her presence. They'd headed off in different directions, each scouring the ground.

At least the detective's car was no longer parked along the road. They could reasonably assume she'd left the area.

Polly circled the tree where she'd stood watching the pathway and the woods surrounding it. Was it really possible for a large hairy creature to blend in with the tree and go without notice?

Not the creature she'd seen. The trees around the

campsite were good-sized ones, but the creature they'd seen, his . . . or her . . . legs had been as big around as some of the trees.

Polly stared upward into the leaves of the tree. Could a Bigfoot be stealthy above the woodland floor?

They were said to be man-apes, so possibly.

Then she lowered her gaze to the ground. What could Connie and Ethan be searching to find? She explored the dirt, twigs, and leaves. Then the mystery revealed itself. She knew exactly what her sister and her son wanted to find.

But how could they? She circled the area where she stood in hopes of finding a location clear of debris. Her search widened with no result. Dead leaves and twigs littered the ground.

When she looked up, she startled and did a one-eighty. How far had she walked from her sentry-point?

Too far.

She was deep in the woods, it seemed, and standing in front of another type of structure, not a shelter, but a hodge-podge of hefty sticks arranged in another type of teepee-like marker that was definitely not nature-made.

In the distance was another and another, as if pointing the way to something, but what?

She did another pivot. Nothing looked the least bit familiar.

Birds sang and chatter rang out from some small creatures, but she didn't hear her son or her sister.

She smacked her head with her hand before pulling out her phone. Reception was iffy but not unheard of in the park, and she did have a few bars. She group-texted with Connie and Ethan.

Several minutes passed with no response.

She looked at the imposing structures and went to the second one. The ground around it had been disturbed, but there were no footprints, which is what she had realized they'd been seeking.

But she'd found something bigger. She moved ahead. The next structure produced the same findings.

Five structures later, she stopped and breathed a sigh of relief.

Just beyond, the lake sat pristine and beautiful.

The soil around this structure, though far enough from the lake to remain hidden, was a little more pliable due to the moisture from the water.

Polly looked around and stopped.

She gasped, took out her phone, and clicked a picture of a large bare footprint. As she'd seen on many of the shows, she carefully placed her covered foot beside it and snapped a picture. Then she removed her foot and snapped another.

As an afterthought, she moved around the structure,

being careful not to step on any other evidence. Looking back, she saw that each structure was in a perfect line. She took another picture.

She moved toward the lake and eyed the waterline. Beyond her and to the left approximately three-quarters of a mile was the boat launch. Now she had direction. Follow the structures back to the first and turn in the direction of the marina and parking lot.

If she didn't know better, she'd think she learned a thing or two from her time in the woods.

She made her way to the first structure and turned in the direction she knew would lead her to where she'd been.

She breathed a huge sigh of relief when she stumbled upon the original tree, but only for a moment. Where were Connie and Ethan?

A twig snapped behind her, and she whirled around. Nothing.

And the forest had gone as quiet as it had been outside of her tent on the night of Reilly Jantzen's murder.

A low grunt sounded from somewhere nearby.

Connie turned a full three-sixty.

Fear held her paralyzed. If that big creature stepped in front of her now, she'd have a heart attack. "Connie," she barely got the word between her lips. "Not funny."

Hurmpf.

Polly leaned against the tree. This wasn't happening to her. "Ethan, not funny. Come out. Now."

Thrashing sounded to her right. Connie and Ethan peeked through the forest. "Got what we need." Connie drew near. "No sign of being followed, huh?"

Whatever she'd heard had not been from those two. They'd been too far away. She had to get them out of this place.

"What did you find?" Polly asked.

"Nothing definitive."

"Let's get home." Polly shivered. "I feel as if we're being watched."

Connie caught up with her. "I've had that feeling since we first arrived, but you didn't see anyone, did you?"

Polly shook her head. The truth would come out later, but right now, she wanted to get home to the safety of her husband's arms.

Once they were on Route 23 and headed back to Ashland, Polly called Marc to give them their ETA. He volunteered to order pizzas and salads and would have them delivered by the time they arrived.

She dearly loved that man, especially since he was averse to "easy meals," declaring that many children had no idea the joys of a homemade sit-down dinner and the family communication it elicited. Fast food deliveries or pickups created a fast-dining, no-discussion experience that allowed parents and children to go their separate ways as quickly as possible.

But her man also knew that sometimes rules could be broken and that broken rules sometimes brought a smile to a kid who didn't get to break them so much.

Marc had the table set, glasses ready, salad in bowls, and the pizza sitting in the middle of their plates. Polly kissed his cheek. "Thank you."

Marc winked. "You all had a very long day. I was getting worried when it started to get dark."

Ethan yawned and stretched. "These two are mad women." He fist-bumped Connie. "We ate breakfast at Down Home Grill, got some good intel, went to the lake, ran into someone scarier than Sasquatch, they went to the bank to talk to Mr. Bastien, we started out to the lake, turned around to eat at Dee's Drive-Inn, ate, and headed out to the lake again."

"A very busy day." Marc motioned for them to sit. He stood and prayed over the food and then joined them. "Why go to the lake twice?"

"Intel, Dad," Ethan explained. "Mr. Bastien and the

guy running Dee's, they were cryptic about Bigfoot being a woman. And we thought that maybe they had a reason."

"Did you figure it out?" Marc bit into his pizza.

Connie lifted her glass of sweet tea in Marc's direction. "We found some shoed footprints, but they could have been from the investigators or anyone curious about the scene. Yeah, they had big feet, but Bigfoot doesn't wear shoes."

"Which is why we went back there." Ethan chomped on a second slice of pizza.

What was? Polly was either dense or being left out of the game on purpose. She didn't like the emotions conjured up by being the third-guy out, so she chose to believe she hadn't grasped what they were trying to tell her.

But she wouldn't ask either. No way she'd admit to her little sister that she didn't understand. Besides, she had kept her own secrets. "Did you take pictures?"

Ethan pulled out his phone from his pocket and stopped. He swiveled his attention between Polly and Marc. "Permission to use my phone at the dinner table."

Marc laughed. "Yes, son. Go ahead."

Polly smiled. "Glad you asked. I have something to share, too."

Ethan pulled up his photos and handed the phone to

Marc who looked and then handed it to Polly.

Polly studied the large shoe print. "Those are utility boots, aren't they?"

"Yes," Connie muttered. "The kind that police wear." She scrunched her face. "Funny thing, though."

"What's that?" Marc wiped his mouth—and unlike Ethan, he used a napkin.

"We were able to see a clear path for whoever walked here, but there weren't a bunch of them. I don't believe this was from the night of the murder."

Ethan grabbed a napkin as well, held it up, and smiled at Polly. He wiped his face. "Makes me think our theory might be right."

What theory? Polly almost asked the question aloud, but pride kept her lips tight and made her hold out her own phone. She swished her finger to the first picture she took. "These photos are much better, don't you think?"

Connie snatched the phone from her and lined up Ethan's phone beside it. She stared at it for a moment and then scrolled, eyeing Polly when she came to the structures. "Where'd you get these?" She flipped back to the first photo and handed both phones to Ethan who gave a low whistle.

Marc took the phones and coughed. He had to clear whatever went down the wrong way before speaking, and when he did, his voice was raspy. "Next to your foot, that bare one looks like it belongs to a Neanderthal."

Polly wiggled her shoulders. "Perhaps it does."

"Where'd you find them?" Connie repeated her question. "Was it around where you were standing guard?"

Polly's face warmed. "No. In all truthfulness, I wasn't on guard duty the entire time. I finally realized that you two were looking for footprints, and I started to look around. I wandered off and actually got lost."

"Way to go, Mom." Ethan now gave her the coveted fist-bump.

"Scroll to the first photo," Connie insisted.

Marc did as she said, and this time, both he and Ethan coughed.

"There are five of them in a row, and they led right to the lake." Polly nearly jumped with glee at the surprise she'd given to her family.

"Why?" Connie sat her pizza slice back onto her plate. "What purpose do they have? I need some Bigfoot instruction here. What does someone want people to believe that Bigfoot is doing here?"

"Experts believe they build these things as a boundary line. 'You, human, you stay over there. We'll stay wherever we want, but so long as you heed our warning, you'll be fine,'" Ethan explained.

"So, I wandered into Old Hairy's territory?" Polly

shivered.

"If you believed in him, you mean." Connie smirked.

"Well, you told an entire restaurant this morning that Old Hairy was involved."

"Yeah, Dad, that's right." Ethan nearly jumped out of his seat. "Folks in the diner were talking about their encounters. They've been seeing him up there a lot lately."

"Or so someone wants others to think." Connie dug into her pizza again.

Polly remained stuck on the fact that she could have inadvertently wandered into a location where she had been warned to stay out. "I thought that maybe they were pointing to a location. I never dreamed they could be a no-trespassing sign."

"We'll go back and take a look tomorrow after we talk with Myrtle."

Polly ate a bite of pizza. She wasn't so sure if she wanted to go back into those woods. Sure, a man could have made those structures. All it would take was an axe, a knife, and some muscle, but she was convinced that short of heavy equipment, the lean-to structure had not been made by a man.

And she hadn't imagined the twig snaps, the eerie silence, and the grunts.

"What did you learn from Bastien?" Marc asked.

Connie pushed her plate away and picked up her tea. "He wasn't very helpful by way of clearing Myrtle and Fred, but we put him on notice that we think he's involved."

Marc cleared his throat. "I asked you to tread carefully, didn't I?" He sat back. "What was I thinking?" He shared a look with Polly that told her he was amused by his own gullibility. "However, there's something that doesn't fit well with me in all of this. Have you wondered why Reilly would accept help from Fred and Myrtle? He'd be suspicious of her reasoning, don't you think?"

Polly had not taken the time to think about that little plot hole in their mystery.

And by the silence coming from Ethan and Connie, the bet was safe that they had not either.

Connie tapped her nails on the table for a long moment before snapping her fingers. "Reilly would have realized that pushing Myrtle away from helping him would arouse more suspicion of him. He had to allow it."

"That sounds good," Ethan agreed.

"Or . . ." Marc raised his eyebrows. "Myrtle and Fred knew what Reilly was doing and threatened to go to the police. They demanded a cut if they helped him search, and when he dug up the money, they got greedy. Perhaps James Bastien was a part of that as well."

Silence again reigned.

"I guess we have a very important question to ask Myrtle." Connie stood and collected the dishes.

Polly joined her in the kitchen, and they worked in silence to clean up.

Finished, they found Ethan had wandered off to bed, and Marc was in the family room with the television on but the sound lowered.

"Ethan's a little disappointed in humanity," Marc filled them in. "Said that my scenario was too perfect to be the wrong one."

Polly sank to the couch. "I'm not giving up hope in my assessment of the Conrads until we have a chance to talk to Myrtle."

"Why don't you three come to the center tomorrow to place the call? I'd like to hear what she has to say, and we have the screen in the conference room. It'll be like she's in the room with us."

"Sounds like a plan." Connie yawned. "I think I'll head up."

She stood, and Polly reached for her hand. "Your patience with my decision is duly noted."

Connie leaned over and kissed Polly's cheek. "Remember when I mentioned that I enjoyed the give and take you and Ethan have?"

"I do."

Connie swung Polly's hand up and back. "I realized that you and I have the same relationship."

Polly scrunched her nose. "I don't see it."

"We're always at each other. Ever since I graduated college, we've been rubbing each other the wrong way. But it's actually comforting to me. Tells me that you still love me. I've spent so much time trying to overcome being the bothersome little sister, especially to you, but the truth is, that's us."

Polly giggled. "I'll have you know that I've never tried to overcome being your bossy big sister, but I think I need to change."

Connie hugged her. "I think not. It's who we are. I would no more want you to be different with me than I would want you to be different with Ethan."

"You trained me well for that interaction."

"But we can pull it together and cooperate for a bit to get through this mystery, can't we?" Connie moved away, and Polly released her hold.

"Yes, we can, and I'm warming to the thought of working with you. I might even renew my Illinois license."

"The Wright Foundation could benefit from that." Connie stepped to the stairs. "Good night."

"'Night," Polly waved her hand.

Marc snuggled down in his chair and patted his lap.

The Visitor Meets Old Hairy

"Come sit with me."

    Polly didn't have to be asked twice.

Chapter Sixteen

Myth Me This

Polly sat at the conference table at the behavioral center. Connie sat beside her. Marc stood over Polly's shoulder, and after showing the adults how much smarter teenagers were these days by setting up and starting the conference, Ethan stood behind his aunt.

Myrtle looked so small and pale in orange. The contrast to the vibrant woman who'd attended the expeditions with her family caused Polly to wince. "How are you?" she asked.

Myrtle's head shook with a slight tremor. "I'm doing as well as can be expected. Never thought I'd be a resident inside a jail, though."

"Myrtle, we have limited time," Connie jumped in. "We're going to ask you some uncomfortable questions, and we may be able to help you if you tell us the truth."

"Of course. Never been one to lie when asked something directly." Myrtle sat up.

"Did you and Fred go on these expeditions in order to obtain the money from Reilly."

"Yes, we did." Myrtle stared into the camera.

Polly held back a gasp, and Marc's grip tightened on her shoulder.

"For what reason did you want to obtain the stolen funds?" Connie continued her interrogation, sounding more like the lawyer than Polly.

"To help Reilly."

Around her, Polly shared a look of dismay with her family. Myrtle was backing up Bastien's account. "To help Reilly find the money?" she choked out.

"Yes, dear." Myrtle smiled. "Don't you see . . .?"

"No, Myrtle," Marc snapped. "Don't you see that allowing him to keep the money was a crime. He may have been acquitted, but your knowledge of the money and the fact that Reilly had it, well, it makes you complicit."

"Complicit in what?" Myrtle questioned. "Marc, dear, we were trying to help Reilly."

"Help him what?" Connie pressed.

"We planned the expeditions so that we had a reason to be in the woods."

"So that Reilly could find the money he misplaced?" Ethan asked.

"Reilly knew where the money was located. He'd always known."

"And you three left it out there for the two months we've been with you, used us as part of the ruse, and you planned to dig it up last weekend?"

"That's right." Myrtle bestowed a warm smile upon them as if they were children in a classroom.

Marc pointed to the clock. "Times running out. We need to get to the important stuff."

"Did you kill Reilly?" Ethan asked.

"Oh, goodness. No, and before you ask, neither did Fred. We were helping Reilly. He was going to dig up the money and give it to us. We were going to turn it in. Reilly couldn't be charged again, you see, because he'd been tried before a jury, but it would have given him some extra padding away from the law. We would have turned in the money, telling them we found it in the woods. We wouldn't implicate Reilly at all."

Connie tapped her red nails on the table. "If you three were the only ones who knew, how did Reilly end up dead? And how did the empty cash box end up at your house?"

Myrtle tapped her finger to her temple. "Think about it. That money box couldn't have held more than a few thousand dollars. Reilly got away with hundreds of thousands of dollars. He was a lot of things, but we came to know that Reilly Jantzen wasn't a fool, Ms. Wright. I suspect that Reilly's partner, wanting to turn suspicion toward us, placed that cash box in our home."

"But it fit the hole." Connie sighed deeply. "The box was in the ground."

"Right where someone was clever enough to leave it and pull it out before or after murdering poor old Reilly."

"So, someone else was aware that Reilly would be digging up the money he stole from the bank?"

"His partner, yes. Only Reilly never shared where he'd put the money."

Polly lowered her hands under the table and tightened her fist. "Who was his partner?"

"He never told us. Said it was best to leave that party out of things. It could get complicated."

"Well, isn't he a right little prophet." Connie blew out a breath.

Polly shouldered her sister.

"Did Reilly ever tell you where he'd buried the money?"

"No, but he said the structure was important."

"Myrtle, did Reilly invent the story of Bigfoot around that lake in order to conceal his true reason for being out there? Did he build that structure?" Marc pulled out a chair and sat.

Myrtle sat up and smiled big. "Oh, no, Marc. Reilly told us he'd discovered it, but he didn't make it. He couldn't have. You saw that thing. And people started reporting sightings of a large creature in the woods before we made our way out there. That's how come I offered the solution to Reilly. Get a group of people together for a Bigfoot expedition and you have a great cover."

"And Fred dressed up as a Sasquatch to further the illusion."

Myrtle's head shook with a negative. "We would never do that. Too many people in these parts have guns. And I wouldn't want to play that kind of a joke on my friends and neighbors. I'd never let my Fred wander around in the woods like that."

"But Reilly, right?" Ethan asked. "He had to, right? That was who they saw?"

"No, Ethan," Myrtle said, her voice soft. "None of us dressed up like Old Hairy."

"Or Old Harriet," Connie breathed. "So, really quickly, Myrtle. The structure, could that be where Reilly hid the money?"

"I only know that the structure is important."

Behind Myrtle, in the glass of the room's door, a

guard peered in.

"We're running out of time. Anything else we need to know?" Ethan asked his family.

"Yes." Polly had almost forgotten what she thought would be a big clue. "Myrtle, when you went back into your tent for the flashlight and toilet paper, I could have sworn something startled you. Was it because Fred wasn't in the tent?"

The door handle turned, and Myrtle looked behind her. She blanched.

"We need to know," Connie insisted.

"I knew Fred wasn't in the tent. He'd been out with Reilly. That's not as important as who was in the tent." Myrtle's shoulders fell.

"Who was that?"

An imposing female guard stood in the door behind Myrtle. "Mrs. Conrad, times nearly up."

"Yes. Yes." Myrtle waved. "Ten more seconds, please."

"You have twenty." The guard winked and left.

Myrtle turned to peer at them again. "James Bastien was in the tent. He was out of breath, and he was terrified."

"Do you think he killed Reilly?" Polly blurted.

Myrtle bestowed on her the kindest, grandmotherly smile Polly had ever seen. "No, dear. I do not."

"Then why was he in your tent?"

"He shouldn't have been." Myrtle shook her head. "I believe he was very, very frightened. Wouldn't you be? Reilly was laying out there dead, and Fred was nowhere to be found."

"Did you learn where Fred had gone?" Connie's gaze drifted to the door behind Myrtle.

Time was running out.

"Yes, dear. He went to hide the cash box in our car."

The door behind Myrtle opened, and the guard stepped forward. "The time is up." Her voice was kind, but she was all business. "That's all folks." She clicked the computer, and the screen went dark.

Ethan leaned over and got them out of the program. "Well, the box wasn't planted in their garage. I thought maybe someone had done that." Ethan slumped back into the chair. "I don't think we can help them. Even if they aren't guilty, they've done themselves in."

Marc held up his hand as if in thought.

They waited in silence.

"Myrtle said that she believes the box was planted and dug up by whoever Reilly's partner is." He stood and paced. "Why would she then admit that Fred hid the cash box in her car?"

Again, silence fell over them.

Polly wracked her brain until a thought percolated.

"Maybe," Polly stood and paced beside Marc, "the partner was spooked by hearing either Fred or even Bastien." She clicked her fingers. "Spooked. Bastien had been spooked. What if he'd been digging the box? What if Reilly surprised him, and he killed Reilly before or after digging it up. He heard Fred coming, and he dropped the box and ran for safety, maybe planning to lie to Myrtle and tell her that Fred killed him. Why was Bastien out there except that he was up to no good?"

Ethan had remained silent. He seemed defeated.

"What is it?" Polly asked.

"Don't you get it? Reilly and Bastien built that structure to hide the location of the money he buried. It's inside, I'm sure. Bastien killed Reilly, and after everything dies down, he's going to go into that shelter, dig up the money, and be home free. We should just let the police do their job from here. Bastien was Reilly's partner from the start."

"No." The single word fell out of Connie's mouth as if she was ordering them to stand down. "There's a problem with that scenario."

"What?" Polly prodded. "Bastien was there." She clicked her fingers like her sister always did. "I'll bet he was the person who was outside my tent. The man is huge. Myrtle said he was out of breath and frightened. That equals the sounds I heard."

Connie shook her head. "I'm sorry, Polly, but I'm not so sure about his involvement in a murder. Something's up with him, but I don't know what. Why would he go into the Conrad tent? He wouldn't have known Myrtle was leaving. And what's to say she wouldn't have screamed out. I would if a man crept into my tent in the middle of the night."

"Crept? Him?" Polly laughed. "And you wouldn't scream. You wouldn't even wake up."

Connie cast her a piercing look. "I would."

"Yeah, right." Polly poked.

"Myrtle would've." Connie ignored her. "By her own admission, Fred wasn't there when she came out. Neither was Bastien when she left the tent the first time. Fred could have used the front flap to exit that old tent. No one would have been suspicious seeing him leave. They'd think he was doing exactly what we were doing. Leaving from the back would be more suspicious. Bastien even being on scene, now that would raise a lot of suspicion. He had to lift up the back and get inside. Myrtle wouldn't have suspected that at all. She'd expect Fred to return the same way he left, and perhaps she was only using the bathroom as an excuse. Fred might have been gone far too long for her liking."

"I hate to admit it, but I think you might be onto something after all." Polly picked up an empty glass from the table and set it on a coaster.

"But why hasn't Myrtle told the authorities that Bastien was there?" Connie continued to voice her thoughts aloud. "She has to be wondering why he was there, and Bastien never admitted his presence to us. He's hiding something, and I think it's more than the location of the stolen money. He has to have been Reilly's double-crossing partner."

They fell silent for a long moment.

Then Marc stood. He went to the phone and punched in an extension. "LouAnne, I've had something come up. Could you cancel my appointments for today and tomorrow? If anyone insists that they need to see someone, ask one of the other counselors to fit them in."

"What are you doing?" Polly reached for his hand.

"Do you think I'm going to let my family solve this mystery all on your own? Let's go home, pack, and go out to stay in Louisa. Tomorrow morning, we're going to that lake, and we're going to find that money."

Connie cleared her throat. "Gang, the money isn't important. If we find that money and turn it in to the authorities, they're going to use it to hang your friends. The evidence will point right to them. Right now, they think Fred and Myrtle were only out there on those expeditions to one-up Reilly. Find the money, tell them Myrtle was helping Reilly, and we have a second double-cross scenario for them to take to a jury."

"But . . ." Ethan smiled big. ". . . we have a suspect to throw into Detective Frasier's lap, and clear our friends, don't we?"

The Visitor Meets Old Hairy

Chapter Seventeen

Setting a Trap

After ordering pizza for a second time, Polly reflected on Marc's dismissal of it as a viable alternative for a sit-down dinner. If she lived in Louisa, Giovanni's Pizza would convince her that it should be served at least once a week.

Two empty boxes from Giovanni's lay open on the motel room's side table. The salad had also been devoured. Her family had eaten while sitting in one of the double bedrooms they would share—Ethan next door with his dad and Polly with Connie.

"That was good." Marc's thoughts seemed to be mirroring hers. "Date night, once a month?" He winked.

"At least." She patted her stomach.

"I'm coming along." Ethan stretched out on the bed.

"No, you're not," Marc and Polly chorused.

"You'll be leaving soon anyway," Connie teased. "I'll have to fly in to annoy your mother."

Five days earlier, Polly might have flinched at the thought, but now, she relished the fact that her sister would even suggest returning and annoying her.

A knock on the door reminded Polly that they were expecting a visitor.

Marc went to the door, peered through the peephole, and opened it.

"Evening," the country drawl sounded from the doorway.

"Detective Callahan," Marc greeted. "Detective Frasier." He led the detectives into the room.

"What do you have for us, folks?" Detective Frasier placed her hands on her ample hips.

Ethan sat up. He moved to sit in a chair next to the small table perched by the window but apparently realized he was expected to show some manners. "Detective Frasier." He motioned to the chair.

"No, thank you." She eyed him. "Folks, what's up with you? Why are you back here and calling us?"

Ethan took the chair and stared at the floor.

Polly couldn't have her son think they weren't in the right here. Frasier acted as if citizen interest was a bad thing. "Detectives, we've come across some information, and we thought it best to let you know."

Callahan moved into the room and stood in front of the darkened television. "Go ahead."

Frasier pursed her lips and cast him a look that Polly couldn't read.

"We've learned that James Bastien may have been an inside man at the bank. He may have known, as Reilly did, where the money was located, and he had been waiting for the right time to free himself of a liability and to gain the money," Marc explained.

Frasier tilted her head. "Your wife and her sister here reminded me that the money wasn't my job."

"When was that?" Callahan straightened.

"When I followed them up to the lake. They told me they were wanting to explore the lean-to. Had me convinced, but I suspect that these three," she waved her hand to encompass Polly, Connie, and Ethan, "were snooping out the murder scene."

"Wouldn't you if your friends were railroaded into jail?" Ethan challenged.

"We have Fred and Myrtle Conrad dead to rights, young man. We found the cash box in their home. How else could it have gotten there if they didn't take it home with them?"

"Maybe they found it empty and figured you'd try to put this on them." Ethan wasn't about to backdown.

He had always had a fierce level of justice within him. "Besides, the cash box wasn't big enough for all that money."

Detective Frasier stood over him, her open legged stance threatening. "And you've seen the box, how?"

Marc cleared his throat.

Ethan looked quickly at his father and then looked away. "I—I didn't, but—but I saw the hole." That was her boy, a quick thinker. "Heck, couldn't have held more than a few hundred dollars."

Detective Frasier didn't move from her position.

Polly had had enough. She moved to Ethan and placed her hand on his shoulder. "Back off." She glared at the bouffant-styled woman.

Frasier hesitated a moment and took a step backward. "You can see why I wouldn't want you involved or want you to involve me and my partner. We have no jurisdiction over the money."

"But you do over the murder. It's your investigation." Connie finally seemed to find her voice. "And we plan to deliver that murderer into your hands tomorrow. We've contacted Bastien. He's meeting us tomorrow morning, and we can get him up to the lake by insisting we know where the money is buried."

Frasier narrowed her eyes. "Do you?"

"No."

At least her sister didn't lie. They may have had a vague idea that may or may not be true, but they had no idea if they'd find it in that vicinity.

"And if he already knows where it is, and if you tell him you know of the location, don't you think that will put you in danger?" Frasier insisted.

"Whether he knows or doesn't know where the money is buried, we could be in danger, but if it gets a real murderer behind bars, I'm for it," Polly jumped in.

Frasier laughed. "The murderers are in jail, and I have no intention of entrapping a man like James Bastien. He cooperated fully with the investigation. He had no idea that Myrtle was working with Jantzen or that she'd double-cross him."

"Detective?" Marc said to Callahan. "Do you concur?"

Callahan hesitated a moment. "Detective Frasier's right. We can't have citizens putting themselves into potential danger. Though, I'm certain that you'll get Bastien out there, and you'll learn that he's a good man."

"So, that's the end of it, folks." Detective Frasier headed toward the door. "Do you understand?"

No one spoke for a moment. Then Marc nodded. "Understood. We'll head home tomorrow morning." He led them to the door.

The detectives stepped outside.

"But you can rest assured, that we'll be contacting the Conrads' attorney so that we can testify on their behalf."

Marc shut the door before Detective Frasier could sputter a word.

"We're going home?" Ethan stood. "That woman just planted her size fourteens on our behinds and pushed us out of the chance to save Fred and Myrtle, and you're going to let her do that?"

Marc grasped his son's shoulders. "Yes, I am. We're not going to buck the police, son. You have a scholarship riding on staying out of trouble, and I have to consider the center."

Connie stood and hugged Ethan. "Your heart is in a good place, but the Wright Foundation can't bear any trouble either. We have a solid reputation, and I plan to keep it that way. Your dad's right. We'll testify on their behalf. If it all works out, our theory will muddy the waters of the prosecution's case."

Ethan nodded. He collapsed onto the bed and turned on the television. A crime documentary played in the background.

Ethan pointed. "Could you see one of these shows do a report on Reilly Jantzen's death with Bigfoot as a suspect?"

They laughed.

Polly and Connie cleaned up the boxes, and Marc took the trash to the motel's dumpster.

Connie and Ethan sat on the bed engrossed in the episode while Marc took Polly's hand and opened the front door. "There's a nice breeze." He slipped his arm around Polly, and she relished the comfort and security.

"And it's so nice and quiet here."

Almost as soon as she said it, the phone rang. "Or was."

Marc stepped away from her and pulled the old-fashioned receiver from the cradle. "Yes?" He listened. "We can do that. Yes. We'll be there. Thank you." He hung up.

Polly stepped back inside and closed the door as Ethan muted the television.

"Who was that?" Polly asked.

"Detective Callahan. He wants us to have Bastien in the woods at ten o'clock sharp."

"Huh?" Connie straightened and climbed off the bed.

"What?" Surely, she hadn't heard right.

"Wonder how he knew that we were meeting with Bastien at a time that makes ten o'clock sharp feasible?" Connie had voiced Polly's concern.

Had Callahan been in on this with Bastien? No. Frasier would have known. Or had they unknowingly informed two murderers of their plans? Would a hapless Detective Frasier be their only hope? "Ethan Reagan, you won't be going into the woods with us."

"Mom!" Ethan rang out.

"Good idea," Marc agreed. "We'll drop you off at the lake before breakfast. You'll stay clear of the woods, and you can call for help if you think we need it."

"Cool." Ethan yawned. "But you all know how I get when I'm hungry."

"We know. We know," the three adults chorused.

Chapter Eighteen

Close Encounters of the Bigfoot Kind

Guilt racked Polly as they let Ethan out of the car, a bag of fast-food breakfast in his hands. He held up the bag and pouted. "I thought we didn't eat this stuff."

Marc waved. "Stay low. Stay safe. We'll park close by, so you'll see us when we return. One time of the bagged stuff isn't going to kill you."

"Not a good choice of words, Marc." Polly sank into the seat with her arms folded. "I'm rethinking this. I'd rather have him with me than to have him out here alone."

"You do understand that if Bastien is desperate enough to kill Reilly, he won't hesitate to take out any other witnesses, right? I don't want him involved in this." Marc gave her a tender look with a bob of his head.

Polly nodded her understanding and remained silent as they drove back to the motel and picked up Connie. Then at 8:55 a.m., they walked into the Down Home Grill to the now familiar welcome and a "Glad to see you back."

International Harvester Man waved. "Still looking for Old Hairy?"

"Not this time." Polly nodded toward a man sitting at a table in the middle of the restaurant. So much for quiet conversation. "We're meeting Mr. Bastien," she told the woman who had come to seat them at a table.

Bastien pushed out his chair and lifted his lumbering bulk as they approached.

Marc shook the man's hand. Bastien pulled out a chair for Connie, and Marc did the same for Polly. They only spoke pleasantries until the food was delivered to the table.

Marc held up his coffee for the waitress to top it off. He thanked her and took a sip. "We appreciate that you took time away from the office to meet up with us this morning, and we think we might know where Reilly Jantzen buried the money."

Bastien sat down his fork and wiped his mouth. "The bank's money?"

"The bank's money." Marc sat down his cup.

"I don't think so, Mr. Reagan. I'm sure that it was

taken up the night Reilly was murdered."

"You mean in the cash box."

Bastien seemed to hesitate. He looked around him and then leaned over the table. "No. That cash box was planted. Why do you think I'm working so hard to get Fred and Myrtle out of this?"

Wait. If Bastien was the killer, why was he confirming Myrtle's story of the cash box? Still, they had to see this through.

The door to the diner opened, absent the usual greeting from the counter. All eyes turned on the newest diners.

Three men had entered. They wore hunting gear, which was unusual enough for the time of year, but their looks—all three of them appeared to be bone weary and maybe frightened.

"What happened to you, son?" A waitress ran to one of them.

They weren't men at all. Only teenagers.

"He's out there." The young man pointed toward the door. "Old Hairy. He's out there at the lake. BJ, me, and Tom, we were camping out, hoping to see him, and we got more than we bargained for." He spoke to the crowd, and he had everyone's attention.

"We set up camp in the woods. We fished for a bit, and we were sitting around the fire."

The waitress stood back, her folded hands to her chest.

International Harvest Man turned his chair so he was in the direct line of sight of the storyteller. "Go on, Vic."

"We heard a whistle and then a response. At first, we thought maybe a whip-or-will was nearby. Then it happened again. It weren't no bird, I tell ya."

"That got our hackles up," another of the youth picked up the story. "And then we heard a knock. It sounded like someone had taken a baseball bat to a tree, but we couldn't tell where the sound came from."

"Then we noticed that everything else had gone silent," the third youth advised.

"But not for long," Vic picked up his story again. "A rock fell between us. A big one. Then another one almost hit BJ."

"What'dya do?" International Harvest Man scooted to the edge of his seat.

"Bill, we didn't know what to do. We got in the tent, and that's when the near boulder landed close by. No man lifted and threw that thing."

"A catapult," Connie interjected.

A rush of pssts and shhs greeted her logical analysis.

"Weren't no catapult, ma'am." Vic moved further into the restaurant. "We would have heard it launch."

Connie thought on that for a moment and then nodded. "Granted. What happened next?"

"The howling." Vic turned to look at everyone. "The ungodly sound filled the air. It triggered the coyotes, and we couldn't hear ourselves think. Seemed as if we were surrounded, and there was no way we could leave. We had no idea where those things were at."

"You stayed out there all night?" Polly could hardly believe that they would. "Where did you camp?"

"There were these five pillar structures, tree limbs leaned together but in a straight line toward the lake. We camped close to them. BJ said he thinks we entered into Bigfoot territory, and they were angry with us."

Bastien had been watching with intense interest, but he stood and pushed under his chair. "Folks, this has been interesting," he addressed Polly and her family, "but I have to be getting back to the office."

"Mr. Bastien, we were hoping you'd join us to look around where my wife and her sister believe the money remains." Marc kept his voice low, but he needn't have done so. The restaurant was abuzz with excitement, and plans were being made to hunt Bigfoot.

This wasn't good. Not good at all. If these people loaded up and headed to the lake, they'd disrupt the planned sting.

Connie took out her phone and tapped the screen.

Polly caught a glimpse of the clock on her sister's phone. They barely had enough time to meet Callahan's 10:00 a.m. deadline.

Marc must have noticed as well. "Will you humor us, Mr. Bastien? My wife's sister is somewhat of a sleuth, and they believe they've figured out where Jantzen buried the stolen loot."

"I'm telling you that it isn't there." Bastien raised his hand, and the waitress came over. "Tilly, I'm paying for the fine folks. Put it on one ticket."

"Yes, sir." The waitress scratched on her pad and handed him the bill.

"We can't let you do that," Marc insisted. "We asked you to join us."

"But you've been working to clear my friends. This is my way of paying back."

"But we can clear them if we can prove that they didn't take the money." Connie bounced her leg, a clear indication she was nervous. "Please come with us."

Time was running out on them.

"Or do you think they did it?" Marc stood. "We're going out there, Mr. Bastien, and I would suggest that if you want to clear your friends, you'll join us."

"Or do you actually believe they're guilty and finding the money will prove it?"

Polly widened her eyes at her sister. She'd just given

Bastien the hole in their theory.

"All right, then." Bastien nodded. "I can give you a half-hour. I have a meeting at the bank at eleven." He looked at his watch. "We'd better hurry."

"We'll meet you there." Marc stood and pushed his chair under. "I need to take a detour. Ladies, go on out, and we'll follow Mr. Bastien up."

Polly and Connie weaved through the crowd and waited for Bastien to pay while Marc detoured toward the area marked "Restrooms." When Bastien met them at the door, he turned to Vic. "I'm glad you're safe. I've seen the creature. She's fierce, and I believe she's deadly."

He held the door open for Connie and Polly and then walked to his car. "I'll head on up and wait in the parking area." He leaned out the window. "But I really do need to make my next meeting."

"We'll be right there," Polly assured while digging into her purse for her own key. Finding it, she opened the door and sat inside.

Connie did the same, taking the backseat. "What is Marc doing taking a bathroom break now."

"Spoken like a woman who doesn't have a man." Polly laughed. "They can't hold it like we do."

"Well, if we'd held it the night of the expedition, we might not have been the ones to discover the body,"

Connie groused.

"Myrtle would have discovered it alone. At least she had us with her. And what were you thinking? You realize that if we find the money, he can now turn it around on Myrtle and on us and claim that we were involved."

"I had to do something to get him to move. Either the man didn't realize he had us, or he's not involved." Connie pointed. "Now, what's he doing?"

Marc had exited the restaurant with Vic and seemed to be in an intense conversation with the kid. They shook hands, and Marc hurried to the car.

"What was that?" Connie asked.

"Insurance." He pulled out his phone, sent a text to Ethan, and they drove off.

Chapter Nineteen

It's Murder Being a Hairy Man

No one seemed to be stirring around the lake as they parked beside Bastien's car, and Polly could not get a line of sight on Ethan. That worried her, but she didn't say anything. They'd told him to lay low, and he was an obedient boy.

What did cause dread to seep into her was the fact that there was no sight of a team of state police. Wouldn't they be milling around on the docks, at the shore, appearing like patrons of the park?

Bastien was sitting in his car, his legs sideways. He bent down, and when he finally joined them, he had changed from his dress shoes into a pair of utility boots. "Glad I had these."

Polly exchanged a glance with Connie. Hadn't they

found a pair of boot prints that large?

Bastien was tall and large, and his shoe size matched. If he stepped anywhere barefooted that would make a print, it was sure to spread a bit larger than the actual span. Sure, Bigfoot prints were said to have different characteristics from humans, but they had not heard the findings of any authorities on whether the print found near the murder scene had been human or not.

Besides, she'd seen Bigfoot prints debunked by the fact that a bear, when walking, would place its back paw in the same spot as the front paw. The outcome was pretty close to what people thought were Bigfoot tracks.

Had the creature they'd seen in the woods been a man and not a thing after all? Had the print she'd found been a bear?

"So where are we going?" Bastien walked beside them.

"To the structure." Connie stepped ahead.

They walked silently using the campground to enter the woods. At the structure, Bastien walked around it. "I don't see where it could be. Nothing's been dug." He rubbed his chin. "Believe me. If this was the location of the money, there'd be holes a-plenty."

Marc went around the opposite side before stepping inside. "Who do you believe would have dug it up?" He began to remove the bedding. A too pungent odor unleashed from the matted mess.

Marc coughed and backed out. "I'm not disturbing that, and I don't think Jantzen did either." He held his hands away from him and shuddered. "Perhaps we need to dig around the outside."

"What makes you think the money is here?" Bastien asked.

"The lean-to has to be a marker," Polly explained. "We believe Reilly didn't lose the money. He knew exactly where it was because he had a marker." She trudged along the outside of the structure and kicked at the dirt with the heel of her hiking boot.

Nothing had been loosed from there.

Bastien shook his head and started down the trail. "There's nothing here, folks. I'm telling you that she got it."

"She, again?" Connie mouthed.

"Mr. Bastien, who is this she?" Marc asked.

Bastien turned slowly, and his eyes widened. He sputtered and pointed behind them.

"Mom?"

The hair on Polly's neck stood up. She pivoted.

Ethan stood with the hairy creature, two shovels in his hands. Its left arm was wrapped around her son's neck.

And in its right hand it held a gun.

Polly started forward. "Let him go!"

"No!" Marc grabbed her.

The creature didn't make a move or a sound.

"What do you want? Let him go," Connie demanded.

"Take me," Polly pleaded.

"Give me the money. I'll give you the kid." The creature's voice could frighten the bravest soul as if a device was being used to both distort and magnify, but clearly whatever was inside the suit was human.

"We don't have the money." Marc stepped forward.

"It's true." Bastien moved in. "They thought it was here, but it's not. We were just leaving. If you'd left the boy alone and watched, you might have realized that. These good people only wanted to clear the Conrads."

"By implicating you." The person inside the costume laughed, and it reverberated through the woods.

Ah, that's how they'd made the howling so realistic.

Connie's hand snaked into Polly's, and Polly turned her attention to her. "Callahan . . ." Connie mouthed.

The creature laughed. "How clever of you."

Connie shook her head, but she remained silent.

"This boy's life depends on you finding the money. Start digging."

"With what?" Polly screamed. Another flaw in their plan became all too vivid. They had nothing to dig up the money. Had they really thought they'd find it without tools?

The creature pulled Ethan with him and pushed him. "Give them to the men," it ordered.

Ethan walked forward and handed the two shovels to Bastien and Marc.

Marc pushed Ethan toward Polly who latched on to her boy with all her might. He wasn't going back to stand by Old Hairy, that was for sure.

"Now dig!" the creature ordered.

Connie took a step back, pulling Polly and Ethan with her, and the creature lowered the gun in her direction. "Where do you think you're going?"

"I'm not leaving my brother-in-law and Mr. Bastien. I'm not a coward like you, hiding behind a mask."

The creature laughed again. "But you've unmasked me, haven't you? I'm Callahan."

Something was very wrong here. Polly shivered. "You can't let us live. We know who you are and what you've done. You killed Reilly Jantzen. You were his partner in the bank robbery. You set up Myrtle and Fred."

"You don't know what I did, Mrs. Reagan." The creature stared. "Dig, boys!" It screeched.

An hour later, both Bastien and Marc tossed down the shovels. They'd dug around the entire structure, and

Marc had even been forced inside.

The pungent aroma was all over him and permeated the air.

The person inside the costume had remained silent most of the time. He'd kept an eye on the men and on the women and Ethan.

The men couldn't continue much longer in this heat. Even Polly was thirsty, and she'd been standing mostly in the shade. She peered through the woods and longed for the lake. Not that she'd drink from it, but the water would feel refreshing.

The beast in front of her had lowered its gun a bit. That costume had to be hot, and the vile creature inside would have to come out for air soon.

She tried to map out the route she'd taken previously when following the structures.

Wait. The structures . . .

The structures . . . five of them . . . each was one structure. Myrtle hadn't been talking about this structure. She'd been talking about one of the structures. She may not have known it, but that had to be it.

"I know where the money is!"

Marc startled.

Bastien held his chest. "I can't do this any longer. I've been having pains for the last ten minutes."

Polly prayed it was only indigestion from the huge

meal and the over-exertion, but too many variables said otherwise.

"Where, Mrs. Reagan?" The creature's voice didn't sound so loud now.

"The lake. I discovered structures that lead to the lake. I'm certain the money is buried under the last one down by the lake. It's easily accessible by walking the shoreline, but it isn't somewhere that most of the park's patrons utilize."

The creature motioned with the gun. "Pick up the shovels, men. Mrs. Reagan, you lead the way. One wrong move, and the first bullet goes into the kid. Got it?"

Vile. Whoever was inside was evil. What would it take to even threaten a young man's life?

Bastien and Marc did as they were told. Bastien leaned heavily upon the handle of the shovel as Polly struggled to find the right path.

The first structure came into view. Polly led them past it and toward the lake.

The creature followed behind them, but not as closely as Polly thought it would.

Polly placed her arm through her husband's as they walked. "The sun by the lake is going to fry what's left of him," she whispered close.

Marc slipped his arm from hers. "Look, Callahan. I'll dig. Let Bastien sit this one out. If Polly's right, I should locate it close to or under the structure."

"In case it's only nearby," Ethan offered, "I'll look around close."

The creature again waved the gun as they entered the clearing. "Get to it then. We wouldn't want old James dying before his time."

"With the bulk that skinny Callahan has to have on to make that girth, he's got to be dying," Polly said to Connie with her back to the creature.

"Whoever's in there, I'm counting on it."

After a time, Marc gave up. "It's not here, Polly."

"That's it!" The creature thundered. "Get over there with them, Mr. Reagan. My patience is at an end. You call yourself amateur detectives."

Connie had peered off into the woods. She nodded at something. "What made you do this? Why'd you partner with Jantzen to rob the bank? Isn't it enough that you have a good job working for the state?"

"A good job? Yeah. Thankless, you mean. And I didn't partner with Jantzen. He partnered with me. This was all my plan."

"How'd he get away with the money?" Connie wasn't letting up.

"He was supposed to hide it, but I never dreamed he'd come out here and bury it in the dirt. A locker—something, but here? Then he stabbed me in the back.

Said he couldn't find it, but he knew where it was. I wasn't going to get it out of him, so I killed him. Figured I'd find it better on my own. I would have, too, but you folks came snooping around." The creature waved the gun again. "We need to get back up into the woods. Best not to let anyone else see."

"See what?" Polly nearly screeched.

"Move!" The creature said but stumbled.

Marc shoved Ethan toward the woods. "Find them," he whispered.

Find who? Polly's heart stopped as the creature straightened and pointed the gun in the direction Ethan had gone.

"No!" Polly screamed.

The creature swayed, shook its head, and fought for ground.

Marc motioned for them to stand their ground, and Polly realized that getting Ethan to safety had been his priority. If they made a run for it, someone was going to end up shot, and the largest target would be Bastien.

The large man grasped his heart but managed to stand upright.

Polly prayed that he'd be able to stay strong.

"Move!"

At the creature's order, they silently took steps past the second structure, the third, the fourth, and then the fifth.

Polly stopped.

Or was the last structure the first structure. She'd taken a class in looking at situations through various paradigms. She never thought she'd find it useful, but a different theory told her that the possibility existed that the structure by the lake could be pointing to the structure in the woods.

She glanced around her.

"There!" She raised her hand toward a large rock. On it was a mark of blue paint. "Marc, that's got to be it."

The creature stopped, swayed, and tried to stay on its feet.

Polly prayed it would topple.

The creature's momentum, the heaviness of the costume, and the apparent heat exhaustion worked against its every effort. The bulk moved to the left and then the right, its legs crumbling with each movement.

The horrid thing folded to the earth.

The gun dropped from its hand.

Polly bent down and retrieved the weapon.

The creature didn't move.

Thrashing sounded through the woods, and Polly backed up.

"Put down the gun!" a man yelled. "Put down the

gun, Mrs. Reagan, and move away."

Polly bent and put the gun on the ground. Her heart thudded as she stood and raised her hands. Had they left one trap for another?

Several men in uniform stepped into the clearing, guns pointed at the creature. Behind them and weaponless stood the three young men from the diner and Ethan.

Polly raised her hands out to her boy so thankful he was alive.

Ethan hesitated.

"Go on." Vic nudged him. "Your momma needs you."

Ethan moved forward, allowing Polly to clutch him to her.

Detective Callahan, in full gear, approached.

"What?" Polly looked from him to the creature and back. "I thought you . . ."

He smiled at Connie. "Good job."

Polly released Ethan. "What did she do?"

"She kept quiet, and the two words she said gave false hope to your abductor who thought it funny that I'd been framed."

Polly looked down at the motionless creature. "I don't understand. Did Detective Frasier really refuse to come out and catch the culprit? I know we caught someone other than Mr. Bastien, but . . ." Polly wanted to offer Bastien a sincere smile of apology, but when she found sight of him, he was on the ground, officers attending him.

Callahan bent down by the creature. "She was here the entire time." He lifted the mask.

Lantana Frasier didn't move. Her head rolled to the side. Her beehive had collapsed; her makeup was running, and she appeared lifeless.

"Is she still with us?" Connie asked.

"All clear," Callahan spoke into his uniform mic. "Send up the EMTs. We have two people down. One appears to be heat stroke. The other could be a heart attack."

"Did you know it was her all along?"

"I suspected, but I didn't want it to be true. We've been partners in the force and in music for a long while, but she made a mistake, and it made me suspicious."

"What was that?"

"She had a shovel of her own in her patrol car. I saw it the night of the murder. Fresh dirt on it, too. When she never mentioned that a shovel was missing from the scene, my antennae were raised. If she'd left it where she'd dug up the cash box, I'd have never been on to her, but I needed more proof. You provided a way to find it out." He nodded toward Bastien and where the paramedics were coming through. "I only hope that letting this play out didn't cost a good man his life."

Polly bowed her head and prayed for the man, shamed that she'd thought the worst of him. Then she wrapped her sister in her arms. "You really are good at this, aren't you?"

"Reluctantly, yes." Connie hugged her.

"It's here!" Marc's voice rang out. "Polly, you're a genius. Detective Callahan. There are several bags here. I suspect they're filled with the bank's money."

A low moan came from the ground beside Callahan.

Lantana Frasier raised her head and then it crashed to the ground.

She was out cold again.

"Guess I'm soloing it at Jimmy Jo's." Callahan shook his head.

The Visitor Meets Old Hairy

The Wrap-up

A Good Legend Never Dies

Polly never thought she'd want to be out in the woods again, and it had taken a week for her to consider going back to Yatesville Lake.

She held out her stick with the marshmallow attached and waited for the fire to catch. Then she tugged it in and blew on the gooey goodness. Pinching it off, she stuffed it in her mouth.

"Glad you could join us," she spoke around the delicious taste bursting in her mouth to her sister beside her.

"How could I refuse?" Connie ate her own burned marshmallow. "Ethan said he wanted me here for his last campout prior to college."

They were all here. Fred and Myrtle, along with

James Bastien, were enjoying nightfall around the campfire with Polly's family, and each had declared the night a celebration for different reasons. The only one not at camp was Marc. He'd caught some fish that needed cleaning, and he'd return soon.

"Let's make a toast." Ethan held up his own toasted marshmallow. "Get it?"

"Got it." Myrtle laughed. "A toast to being vindicated."

"Here. Here." Fred raised his stick. "And to being free."

"Health and the return of the money," Mr. Bastien toasted. "Sure glad that the only problem was indigestion, but don't tell my wife that I'm eating these. She has me on a strict diet."

"To college," Ethan declared.

"To changes," Polly saluted him.

"Those are the same two things," Myrtle challenged.

"No." Polly fixed another marshmallow on to her stick. "After Ethan goes off to college, I'll be working with my husband at the behavioral center." She smiled at Connie. "It was my sister's idea."

Connie leaned over and hugged Polly. "I'm so glad you won't be sitting at home alone."

"What about you, Aunt Connie?" Ethan made his

stick ready as if to battle Polly for position in the fire.

"Not on your life. My marshmallow's at risk." Polly touched his stick in warning. "Back off, boy."

"I'm toasting my sister and her family." Connie laughed. "They're funny and actually pretty great to be around."

"I have a question." Polly speared James Bastien with an intense gaze. "Why were you out here the night of the murder?"

Bastien looked to the Conrads. "I was part of their plan. Reilly was to dig up the money, give it to Fred, and Fred was going to hand it off to me. I would then take it to the bank to wait for Monday morning. No one was to know I was there. We suspected that Reilly's partner was watching. Reilly wouldn't identify the person. He said our knowing would put us in danger. But we suspected his partner was Frasier, or Bigfoot Frasier as we'd called her when she played on Fort Gay's girls' basketball team. I had to remain stealth, so I was up in the woods before any of you arrived."

"Big Foot—her—" Polly sputtered and stopped. "You were trying to warn us."

"Yeah, I gave a call over to my buddy at Dee's when I saw you heading in that direction. I asked him to place a bug in your ear as well."

Polly looked to the heavens. "We really were

clueless, huh?"

"You were, Mom." Ethan chewed his marshmallow and spoke at the same time, earning a glare from her. "Aunt Connie and I talked about the way they both said her. The only her we could come up with was Detective Frasier."

"But you didn't tell me." Polly narrowed her eyes in her direction.

Connie bumped her. "Not purposely. You seemed to be keeping up with us. We didn't know you didn't have a clue."

Polly scrunched her nose at her sister and turned back to the others. "And what exactly happened that sent you into Fred and Myrtle's tent?"

Bastien shifted uncomfortably. "You won't believe me."

"Try us," Connie pressed.

"Bigfoot."

"Bigfoot Frasier, you mean?" Ethan looked around him as if he expected to be the only one not in on a joke.

"No, son. Bigfoot. All seven and a half feet of him. I found Reilly's body. I was bent over him. I heard someone coming through the woods, and I stood up because I expected Fred would be coming along to give me the money."

"What happened?" Ethan stared with rapt attention.

"I smelled him first. Smelled like your dad did when Frasier made him get into the lean-to. My eyes watered. Then I caught movement by the tree, just the slightest flinch, and I realized that what I thought was a tree trunk was the creature's foot. I trailed my gaze up his body, and he and I stared at each other for a long moment. He looked down at Reilly and back to me.

"About that time, Fred came upon me. I looked to him and when I looked back, Old Hairy had departed, and that's all I could think to do. I left poor Fred standing there in the path to fend for himself."

"You were the one outside our tent, right?" Connie reached for a bag of chips sitting nearby.

Bastien shook his head. "I don't think so. I skittered to the back of that old familiar thing that belongs to Fred and Myrtle. I was nowhere near your tent."

Connie straightened with her mouth hanging open.

"What'd you do, Fred? Was that you outside the tent?" Ethan questioned.

"I don't believe so. I didn't go back to the tent. I hung out in the woods and slipped in with you all when the police arrived. After James left, I prayed over Reilly. I had no idea what James had seen, but I don't doubt him one minute." He chuckled. "If I'd known he'd dived into the tent with Myrtle, with my suspicions, there might have been a scuffle. I had no way of knowing if James had killed our friend."

"Friend?" Connie questioned. "Why would you consider a bank robber a friend?"

Myrtle reached for Connie's hand. "Honey, Reilly was more than a bank robber. He was a man loved of God, a man who sat in our church one night, frightened and alone. Fred went to him, and Reilly said his life was in danger. He suspected he'd be killed, and he wanted to make things right. Fred showed him he could do more than that. He could get his life right with God. Then we'd help him get his life right with the law."

Polly looked to the heavens. "Thank you, Myrtle and Fred. I needed the reminder that when we sin, we have Someone who will accept us and forgive us. You showed Reilly what that looked like."

They sat in silence for a long moment.

"The murder weapon is still a mystery," Connie mentioned out of the blue.

"No, dear. I've heard that traces of Reilly's blood were found on the butt of Lantana Frasier's gun."

Polly wrapped her arms around her. "The gun she held on us, the one she would have used to shoot us. Why didn't she just shoot Reilly?"

"We would have heard the gunshot." Connie snapped her fingers.

"Listen." Myrtle put her hand to her ear as if

straining to hear.

"What?" Ethan stood and looked around.

"The woods have gone quiet." Myrtle stood beside him.

Fred, James, Connie, and Polly came alongside.

A soft whistle cut the air to their left.

"Dad!" Ethan called. "Not funny."

Another whistle sounded from the right.

No one moved.

Swack. Wood hit wood.

Polly spun around her trying to determine where it came from. "Marc, not funny."

Another whack sounded in the distance.

Whoop.

A vocalization came from near the camp.

Whoop. The sound was even closer now.

Polly tugged Ethan to her.

He gently pulled away. "Mom, it's Dad. It has to be."

"So, you don't believe Mr. Bastien saw a Bigfoot?"

"Nope." Ethan stepped toward the woods. "I believe he saw Bigfoot Frasier in her costume after she killed Reilly."

"No, son," Bastien declared. "No way she got out of that suit, got freshened up, and got here in her patrol car with the other investigators. I saw the real creature. He's out here."

Leaves moved and an object fell at Polly's feet.

She jumped back and stared at a large rock. "Marc! Not funny."

Stomping and a grunt sounded.

Polly looked at the others. They stood stock-still.

"Oh my," Myrtle gasped. "He's a big 'un." She pointed.

Polly lifted her gaze in that direction.

A creature stood between two trees. It swayed as the one they'd seen the day of Reilly's murder had done.

Fred and James bounced their girth against each trying to move away.

"Marc Reagan. This is not funny!" Connie rushed forward.

The creature stopped and seemed to startle. It lowered its body and raised up, emitting a howl that seemed to go right through Polly.

How had Marc gotten his hands on that suit? Or was someone else playing a trick on them—one of the teens? Wouldn't the suit Frasier wore be evidence?

Was someone else in the woods around Yatesville Lake pretending to be a Bigfoot?

Then the stench hit her, and she turned to run, finding herself behind the others who had jumped up to flee.

"Stop!" Marc came into view.

"It was you!" She couldn't figure out how he'd done it, but it had to be him. Had he had co-conspirators like Detective Callahan or the three teens?

"Wasn't me, Polly. I swear."

Everyone gathered around him, near the firepit. "But are you sure you want to run off into the path of others?"

After several minutes of indecision, they settled down in their chairs, and Marc used the fire to fry up the fish.

"Dad, do you think that was Old Hairy?" Ethan bent down beside him.

"I think it's a mystery we have yet to solve." Marc butted his shoulder against Ethan's. "And we'll have to plan future camping trips out here to see if we can get to the bottom of it."

"Can I come, too?" Connie asked.

"Sure." Ethan stood. "Everyone can. We'll call ourselves Old Hairy Researchers, and I can use that time wisely while working toward my degree."

Marc swiveled but didn't stand. "You think you can counsel a Bigfoot?"

"No, but I can use my cryptozoology major to find the definitive answer."

Marc didn't speak for a long moment, and then he

stood and smiled. "Sounds like a plan." He dished out the fish and sat beside Polly.

"You really don't mind if I don't follow in your footsteps?" Ethan stared at his father.

"Son, so long as you're happy, success will follow in whatever study you go into. I'm just happy that I have you and your mom."

Polly leaned against her husband. "Do you really believe that was Old Hairy?"

Marc touched his head to hers. "No. I think someone caught wind that we were going to be out here, and they played us."

Polly relaxed.

"But just in case," Marc whispered to her, "I left some of my fish over by one of those trees as a peace offering."

The Visitor Sees a Ghost

Preview by Lill Kohler

"Mom, you've got to be kidding." The twins echoed one another on their conference call.

"Well. I'm not." Kimberly expected that response from Cory, but not Lori. A deep breath later she continued, "I got a great deal on the place. It's empty so I can move in as soon as I'm done signing the papers, and I needed a change. I'm sorry if neither of you like the idea of me moving so close to you, Cory, but I need to be near family. And this area of Central Michigan, around Jackson and Vandercook Lake, is quaint and peaceful. Just what the doctor ordered, so to speak."

"It's not that, Mom," Cory took a deep breath and exhaled slowly. "You bought a house sight unseen."

"I saw it. When your Aunt Connie came up here to initiate the foundation fundraiser that she's doing next week, I came with her." Not that she actually toured the place, but she had seen it.

"Since when are you friends with Aunt Connie?" Cory scoffed.

"Well, she made me come." True that she and her baby sister hadn't always been on the best terms, but this time she'd found a blessing from her sister's position.

"But still." Lori chimed in again. "A fixer-upper? You?"

Kimberly counted to ten. She reminded herself it would take time for everyone to see she could single-handedly tackle this house and a move successfully. Soon they would realize fifty-two years of mistakes and hasty, lack-of-knowledge decisions were lessons learned. She could do this. "I saw pictures of the interior online. And my agent did a virtual tour with me. You know, with her phone. I liked what I saw. In this market I was afraid to wait."

Her phone was silent for so long she thought she'd lost the connection.

"Kids? Are you there?"

"I'm here." Lori responded.

"Cory?"

"I'm here, Mom." He huffed. "When do you close on it?"

"In half an hour. I'm standing in the doorway right now. So, not totally sight unseen."

"Now?" Cory questioned, followed by silence.

"Cory, how about meeting for dinner at six, after the closing?" She cleared her throat. "Lori, honey, I know you can't come because of that big project you're working on. We'll miss you. Cory, I'll bring pictures. Lori, we'll send them to you. Ah, my agent seems a bit skittish right now. Need to go. Love you both. Talk to you later." Kimberly clicked off before they could protest again and blew out a cleansing breath.

Her agent was pacing while wringing her hands.

"Denise, what has gotten into you?"

"Didn't you hear that noise when I opened the door?" Her widened, light brown eyes flittered about in search of something.

Kimberly placed her hand on Denise's arm. "I did. This house is old. Look at the floorboards and walls. It's going to creak . . . have old noises."

"Listen. I want you to be happy with whatever you buy." She stepped back toward the front door. "You have enough money, and there's no rush." She cleared the threshold into the mud room. "I don't want you to have buyer's remorse."

Kimberly started to follow but then eyed the dimly lit interior. She shook off the skittishness. Whatever Denise had heard wouldn't change her mind. She stepped into the mud room and crossed her arms over her middle. "You're beginning to sound like my twins." She hesitated, closed her eyes and sighed. "They think I spend money foolishly. Wasting it on junk. That I make bad financial decisions one after another. Granted I have done that in the past." She paused a moment to take in the words she'd just spoken. "Probably why they think I can't make it on my own. That I'll end up broke with nowhere to go."

Denise's mouth gaped farther with each statement. "Kimberly, I didn't mean to imply that."

Kimberly shook her head. "Sorry, I'm tired of being accused of being gullible and incapable."

Denise sighed. "Kimberly, this house, well, it's just that, there are rumors that . . ."

"I know it needs work." Kimberly smiled as she looked back at the unusual Victorian flared gables on the huge three-story lakefront house. Bends, cut-ins, crevices, and windows, lots of windows, from the basement to the attic, spoke of the time it would take to renovate. The one thing she wouldn't change was the deep beige color accented with brown trim and shutters. "But I think that's what I need right now." She walked toward Denise's car.

Denise shook her head. "Very well. But don't say I didn't warn you."

Fay Lamb

Stay Tuned for The Visitor's Next Trip

Scan QR code for a direct link for purchase.

℘203

From the Story
Leaf Me Alone by Julie B Cosgrove

A long-lost child . . . and secrets that insist the lost remain lost!

Word spreads through town about the genealogy researches of Shannon, Bailey, and Jessica. So far, it's been a fun hobby and an eye-opening experience as they helped to solve two murders. But when old Mrs. Perkins, their Bible study leader, wants to hire Shannon and her husband Jayden to find her long-lost nephew, the couple soon learns that moving forward along the Perkins family tree may leave them dangling out on a limb . . .

And someone is holding a saw!

Special Thanks

Thank you, Annie Trosper Moore, for utilizing your extraordinary proofreading skills to ferret out so many of those pesky errors I overlook.

And thank you to Marji Laine for the hard work and all the time you put into The Visitor series, and well, for also allowing me to put Ms. Professional Connie out in them there woods of Kentucky where my hillbilly kin roam.

About Fay Lamb

Fay Lamb is the only daughter of a rebel genius father and a hard-working, tow-the-line mom. She is not only a fifth-generation Floridian, she has lived her entire life in Titusville, where her grandmother was born in 1899.

And, yes, Fay is an avid fan of all things Bigfoot. In fact, Sasquatch has instilled in her this bit of wisdom: "Believe in yourself even when no one else does."

If you'd like to catch up with Fay, visit her at her website, on Amazon, Goodreads, and Twitter. Also, Fay has become a "novel" gardener, and she shares her adventure in her newsletter, Tales from the Azalea Garden. You can sign up for her newsletter on her website.

Links to Social Media:

Website: https://faylamb.wixsite.com/website

Twitter: https://twitter.com/FayFaylamb

Newsletter Sign Up:

https://faylamb.wixsite.com/website/contact

Goodreads: https://www.goodreads.com/FayLamb

Amazon Central: amazon.com/author/faylamb

Also by Fay

The Amazing Grace series
offers life-changing (and life-altering)
suspense.

Mullet Harbor, Florida
has a cast of quirky
character. Their mishaps
make for hysterical and
heartwarming romance.

The Ties That Bind series matches the most unlikely of friends trapped in circumstances requiring unexpected faith for a glimmer of hope.

Serenity Key Saga
How can one man save the town he loves when he's the reason for the destruction?

Thank you
for reading our books!

Please consider leaving a review for the author
on the purchase page for this book.

Look for other books
published by

P

Pursued Books
an imprint of

W

Write Integrity Press
www.WriteIntegrity.com

www.ingramcontent.com/pod-product-compliance
Lightning Source LLC
Chambersburg PA
CBHW072057170626
46813CB00004B/1388